TEMPTED BY DARKNESS

The Wolf Pack
Book Three

by
Avery Gale

Copyright November © 2015 Avery Gale
ISBN 978-1-944472-25-2
All cover art and logo © Copyright November 2015 Avery Gale.
All rights reserved.

Cover by Jess Buffett
Published by Avery Gale Books

Thank you for respecting the hard work of this author.

This is a work of fiction. Names, places, characters and incidents either are the product of the author's imagination or are used fictitiously and any resemblance to any actual persons, living or dead, organizations, events or locales are entirely coincidental.

No part of this book may be reproduced, stored in a retrieval system, or transmitted by any means without the written permission of the author and publishing company.

WARNING: The unauthorized reproduction or distribution of this copyrighted work is illegal. Criminal copyright infringement, including infringement without monetary gain, is investigated by the FBI and is punishable by up to 5 years in federal prison and a fine of $250,000.

If you find any books being sold or shared illegally, please contact the author at avery.gale@ymail.com.

Dedication

Dedicated to the best readers an author could ever dream of...thanks for reminding me daily why writing is the best job in the world.

Chapter One

Kit paced a path in front of the leaded glass windows making up one wall of her husbands' office as she let the events of the day replay through her mind like a movie on a continuous loop. After Tristan's announcement that his wife, Angie, was missing, the entire estate had erupted into a level of chaos, the likes of which, Kit had never seen before. And honestly, that was saying a lot since she was almost always in the thick of everything that caused anything remotely resembling chaos at the Wolf Pack's estate. She'd frustrated Jameson and Trev so often they'd often joked that she'd been forced to stand most of the first year after they'd been mated because she'd gotten so many spankings.

The restless energy pushed her to pace faster and she couldn't decide if it was a reaction to what had already happened, or anticipation of future events. As a "magical", she had always been particularly sensitive to extreme emotions and, right now, she felt as if she was trapped in the seventh level of hell. All around her people were making calls, shouting instructions, and worrying about her friend. Angie Wolf-Michaels was the younger cousin of Kit's husbands and pack Alphas, Jameson and Trevlon Wolf. At five foot seven, Angie towered over Kit, but then most of the shifters in the wolf pack made Kit look like she'd been cheated out of more than a few inches in height.

Angie's slender build, willowy grace, long blond hair and chocolate brown eyes made her look young and vulnerable despite the fact she was a well-respected pediatrician who had graduated from medical school when she was only twenty-two. Knowing her friend was missing felt like acid churning in Kit's stomach.

Glancing over to the corner of the large office, Kit watched as her vivacious grandmother and Cecil, a wizard from the Supreme Council, spoke animatedly on their cell phones. Kit felt a nervous laugh bubble up from deep inside and knew it wouldn't matter how much she tried to tamp it down, nothing would keep the ill-timed sound from escaping. Damn, she'd always had the deplorable habit of laughing when she was nervous and that usually meant she laughed at the worst possible moments. For years her mom had sworn she was simply being disrespectful and while it was true she'd been more than disrespectful as a teen, she had always known this was something entirely different. Her grandfather had been the only one who hadn't judged her for any of her idiosyncrasies and his unconditional love was what made losing him one of the difficult periods of her life. When he'd reached out to her from the other side recently, it had renewed her spirit in a way she hadn't been fully able to explain to anyone. And when she'd found out he and her spitfire granny still talked regularly, it had made his absence more bearable.

As usual, her grandmother was dressed outlandishly. Her high-top sneakers kept changing colors, not flashing abruptly with each step like so many of the kids' shoes Kit saw in stores—no, these had waves of moving color. They reminded Kit of the digital high definition signs in Times Square—hell, they'd probably hypnotize most people. Shaking her head, she turned her attention to the elderly wizard who reminded Kit of Professor Dumbledore in the Harry Potter movies.

Cecil Owen had shown up at the Wolf Pack's estate to check on a young wizard the shifters had been sheltering. Having recently turned sixteen, Braden had come into his full powers, but he was still untrained so no one really knew the full extent of his powers yet. Kit had worked quite a lot since her mother had brought him to the Wolf Pack's estate and she'd seen first-hand how quickly Braden picked up and mastered new skills. She was envious of his almost immediate mastery of spells—hell, he hadn't blown up a single thing in all the time she'd known him. Kit on the other hand often incinerated things without even trying. As an energy conduit, Kit could draw power from the people and objects around her and then focus it with pinpoint—usually, okay occasionally—accuracy.

Kit studied the pair until she figured out what had been bothering her about their little pow-wow. She wondered why their magic didn't affect their cell phones—hell, half the time when she picked hers up it lit up like a Christmas tree. The damned thing didn't want to download messages until she touched it and that was a glitch no one had been able to figure out. When she'd taken it back to the store where she'd purchased it, the two young men she'd talked to had looked at her like she was insane—*as fucking if. I could certainly show them insane. Good Lord of the lepers, look at this place. Wolf shifters, witches, wizards, and a partridge in a pear tree. Oh alright, a member of the Supreme Council on Magicals, but still.* Trevlon's laughter sounded over her shoulder and she let out a squeak of surprise.

"I'm sorry, baby. I didn't mean to startle you, but you were broadcasting your stress pretty loud, so I decided to check on you." Trev's warm breath brushed over the shell of her ear as his arms tightened where they were banded beneath her breasts. As twins *and* Alphas, Jameson's and Trevlon's telepathic abilities were particularly strong, and their abilities weren't limited to each other. Their ability to hear her thoughts had been one of the hardest parts of their relationship for Kit to adjust to. The more time they were together, the stronger her own abilities were becoming, but at times like this, having her husbands hear her thoughts still seemed like a terrible invasion of privacy. "Don't be angry, Kit. You really were sending it out loud and clear." When she looked around the room at several of the other shifters surrounding her, she noticed they nodded in silent agreement. *Drown me.* "No can do, I love you far too much, baby. And besides, I have big plans for you later tonight, although those do involve you being very, very wet."

Kit opened her mouth to protest, she had every intention of leaving as she got confirmation the Supreme Council would see her. Every time she even thought about her spirited friend being exposed to the dark side of magic, she shuddered in revulsion. Kit might have managed to send Damian behind the sealed portal, but there was no doubt he was responsible for this. Damian might not have kidnapped Angie himself, but no one doubted he was the one calling the shots.

The night she'd aimed her powerful magic at Damian, she'd simply been trying to defend Jameson and Trevlon. Hell, it wasn't like she had known what she was doing at the time, she'd just been monumentally pissed off and protecting her men. Her grandmother had been trying to figure out how she'd managed to vaporize the evil wizard who had been trying to recruit her, but so far no one had been able to unravel specifically how an untrained witch had managed such a powerful act. All of Granny Good Witch's training sessions had made the past several months more than a little taxing. After Kit blew up a big bowl of goo during one lesson, the household staff banned her from the kitchen. In an effort to keep peace, Jameson had built a fully equipped *lab* a safe distance from the house. The small building had state of the art fire safety equipment and all the comforts of a guest cottage for her granny's extended visits. But both her mates had insisted the small building's best feature was its location—because it was still on the estate where they could watch out for her safety.

Kit still struggled with the fact she would continually be in danger until Damian had been destroyed—giving that ass hat so much credit and power just grated on her nerves. Damian's brother, Devin, would need to be dealt with as well, but Kit had a gut feeling he was slowly realizing he was fighting for the wrong side. Or perhaps he was simply tired of being his brother's lackey?

Looking up to see Marcus Hines watching her made her wolf growl in frustration. Kit didn't get to shift and run nearly as often as she'd like, and she felt that restless energy begin to surge back to the surface as she looked at the man who had kept so many secrets from his friends. She'd seen the disillusioned expressions on the faces of the two men she adored when they'd discovered the friend who they had considered a mentor all these years was actually a wizard.

Both Jameson and Trev had tried to shield her from their feelings, but they hadn't been able to hide the cloud of betrayal she'd seen move through their eyes when the scope of his deception had been revealed. Why Marcus hadn't disclosed his association with her grandparents, particularly his friendship with her grandfather, still troubled Kit. Something about the man had always bothered her, and she feared there were still secrets lurking in Marcus's soul.

All of her anxiety seemed to drain away when Trev turned her into his arms, pressing her tightly against his chest in the way he knew always brought her back from the edge. "Baby, we'll deal with Marcus—trust me. He is not yours to worry about. Don't let him take up any space in your head." He pressed kisses to the top of her head and sighed, "To be honest with you, I don't understand it either. And I'm angry. He knew we were searching high and low for our mate. He knew all along where you were and he didn't tell us your name or where to find you. A part of my heart is seriously pissed that we lost so much time together, but another part knows all things happen in their own time. I remember our mother telling us time and again as we grew up, I always thought she was merely trying to teach us—well, mainly it was me she was trying to teach, but the lesson in patience was always directed at both of us. Obviously Jameson did a better job of figuring it out." She loved the way his eyes softened whenever he spoke about his mother. It was obvious that both of her mates had their mother and both of their fathers very much. Kit's heart melted a bit more every time they mentioned their parents. She heard the longing in his voice when he softly added, "But now I have to wonder if this wasn't what she was trying to warn us about."

Jameson and Trevlon's mother and two fathers had all been killed while defending their sons. Kit's mother and grandmother had been there too, helping the Wolfs protect the young men, but the seventeen year olds had been locked in a closet by their mother so they'd only gotten the briefest glimpse of the witches who'd come to their aid. Kit's mother, Carla Harris, had been so seriously wounded during the showdown she'd almost died. And seeing her mom's struggle to survive had caused Kit to turn away from magic for many years. Kit had always known becoming mated would bring on her magical powers so she'd avoided any situation she thought held even a remote possibility she might meet her future mate—oh yeah, like the plague she'd avoided them. And then, a simple decision to go dancing changed her life forever.

She didn't have any desire to return to her old life, but there sure were times she wondered what the hell she'd gotten herself into. Her mates were not only the Alphas of their pack, they were also Doms. The two of them had awakened needs in her that she hadn't even known were there. They'd not only known she belonged to them as a mate, they'd also recognized her as a sexual submissive, and they'd known exactly how to unlock that side of her.

Looking up into Trev's dark eyes, she smiled ruefully. She knew her men weren't going to be happy about her plans, but the sooner she started, the sooner Angie would be home. There wasn't a doubt in Kit's mind that Angie had been taken by someone working for Damian. And that meant it was intended to get to Kit or Braden—likely both. "About that promise about later—you may need to hold that thought. If Cecil can arrange an emergency meeting of the council, I'll be leaving right away." When he frowned she pulled his face down and kissed the crinkle between his brows. "Please don't worry, I'll keep you posted and—"

Before Kit had been able to process what was happening, Trev had grabbed the collar of her sweater, yanking it to the side and biting down on the exact spot where he'd bitten her during their mating. He didn't break the skin, but his message was unmistakable. His growl sent shockwaves of arousal through her entire body and she knew the instant the scent of her arousal hit him because the tone deepened. He pressed her against the cool glass at her back until the hard length of his erection was impossible to ignore as it pressed against her. "Mate, you would be well advised to speak very carefully for the next few minutes unless you want everyone in the room to see how I'm planning to remind you exactly who you belong to. The shifters won't mind, but the humans and magicals might be a bit shocked by the sight of my brother and I fucking you at the same time, don't you think? They might not take kindly to the fact one of us will sink as deep into your pussy as possible while the other presses through the tight ring of your ass. And imagine their surprise when you light up everything flammable in the room because we didn't take time to place candles on every flat surface."

Kit could feel her heart racing and knew she was nearly panting with need. *Damn he knows just how to flip that switch.* "Of course I know. You are my mate. It is my job to know exactly how that brilliant mind of yours works. But even more importantly, it is my pleasure to know in precise detail how to bring your lovely body over to my way of thinking. And, baby, I can smell exactly how well my plan is working." Kit felt her entire body mold to his and suddenly nothing sounded so important that it couldn't wait for a quick round of werewolf games. "Just let those thoughts of quickies slide right on out of your mind, baby, because that isn't at all how this is going to work. I'll be accompanying you on this little lobbying trip you have planned. Jameson will stay and run things on this end. We won't ever leave our children without one parent safe at their side."

Kit felt her heart melt at his sweet words. Losing all three of their parents at the same time had left the young men adrift, and she loved the fact they were taking steps to ensure Ryan and Adana were never put in a similar situation. Just as she was ready to give in to the desire coursing through her blood, she heard Braden speak behind Trev's back, "Geez, man, getta room already. There are kids present you know."

Trev's growl was tempered by the smile tugging at the corners of his lips, "Pup, I think you and I need to have a chat about your timing because it certainly needs work." Trev turned and pulled Kit against his side so they faced the room and she tried to bring her raging desire under control. She watched Cecil switch off his phone then close his eyes, as if he was gathering the strength to deliver bad news. Her knees started to sag, but Trev's voice moved over her, "It isn't as what you think, baby, hang on."

Sure, she'd moaned and groaned when she'd first mated the Wolf brothers about how intrusive their telepathic abilities had seemed—they'd looked to her like a major invasion of not only hers, but everyone else's privacy as well. But, right now, in this very moment, it all seemed worth it.

Chapter Two

Ruby Stone was standing close enough to Cecil to hear the frustration in his voice as he'd spoken on the phone to various members of the Supreme Council. By the time he'd finally hung up she could have sworn she actually saw steam coming from his ears. *Shazbat, he looks pissed.* Catching the thought, Ruby sighed, damn it all, she was going to miss that kid. Robin always made her laugh and he never complained or asked her when she planned to stop calling him by his various character names. She'd often called him Mork just to get him to launch into the role anytime their paths crossed.

Over her very long lifetime, Ruby had known many actors, but he had certainly been one of the most talented. Anyone who could bring that kind of joy to those around him had to be one of the bright lights from the other side. Even though her husband assured her he was still entertaining, just on the other side of the veil, it was still a shame the world lost him so soon.

"I swear that council is made up of some the most unreasonable people to ever walk the face of this planet. They simply don't understand all the long reaching implications of this young woman's abduction. They will meet with us day after tomorrow, which works for travel with Trevlon, but by that time I have a feeling my esteemed colleagues are going need shields worthy of asteroids to protect them from Kit's ire." Cecil had closed his eyes and Ruby could feel him pulling energy from around him in order to face Kit and the other members of the Wolf Pack who had gathered in the large room.

Ruby chuckled, "You know her well. That red hair should be a warning, but it's not usually enough." Ruby had seen Kit go from dead calm to full outrage in under five seconds, but it had always been in defense of others. The prophecy had described her spirited granddaughter perfectly, and everyone who knew Kit had been convinced years ago that she was the one they'd been waiting for. Kit was destined for greatness, Ruby simply hoped at the end of the looming battle, Kit emerged as a living legend rather than a hero who perished in battle.

Jameson leaned over Ruby's shoulder and whispered, "You and me both, Granny Good Witch. You and me both."

🐾 🐾 🐾

JAMESON LISTENED AS Cecil explained the Council's response. It was easy to see the wizard was at his wit's end, but he was trying very hard to be diplomatic for Kit's sake. It wasn't working, but the old guy was giving it a valiant go anyway. Jameson was trying to divide his attention between Angie's mates and his own, it was going to be a draw which of the three of them spiraled out of control first. Personally his money was on Kit.

Tristan and Nick Michaels were good men, Jameson valued their opinions and contributions to the Wolf Pack, but he was also keenly aware of their one and only weakness—and that was his brilliant, but mouthy cousin, Angie. The three of them had been mated for several years and

Jameson knew they were anxious to start a family but Angie's intense work schedule always seemed to be throwing out roadblocks. Both men had reached the end of their tolerance and had recently talked to him about using his Alpha status to reassign her to the pack. Jameson and Trev had already reached the same conclusion, but they'd put off speaking with Angie until they could get things settled with Braden—and that delay was certainly a decision he regretted now.

The truth was, he simply hadn't seen this coming and he was usually very good at predicting behavior. They had all expected Damian to order that Kit be brought to him by any means necessary, so they'd been using all their resources to protect her and the twins. They hadn't considered a collateral attack, and that's what this seemed to be. Snatch Kit's friend—a woman everyone knows she loves like a sister, and she'll do whatever you ask to get her back. Jameson watched as Tristan's attention was drawn down to the screen of the monitor in front of him. "Holy shit, Kit, come take a look at this." As the Chief of Security for the Wolf Pack and its surrounding estate, Tristan was usually the epitome of professionalism, so whatever he'd seen had been worthy of interrupting Cecil, a man they all liked and respected.

Kit moved behind him as Jameson and Trev stepped up to flank her. "Watch this. What you're seeing is from the hospital's security feed—no, don't even ask how I got it." And then, just as a woman walked through the sliding glass doors of the lobby, Tristan pointed to the screen, "Isn't that your mom?"

He and Trev both leaned in for a closer look, but Kit just laughed. "No, it isn't." When they all turned to stare at her, she smiled but it didn't reach her eyes. "My mother is a photo-phobe or whatever you call a person who refuses to have their picture taken. If that had been Carla Harris, we wouldn't be looking at this because she would have put out a huge pulse of electromagnetic energy as the outside doors slid open, instantly sending all the cameras into a tailspin that would have made them look as if they'd gone haywire. You'd have found nothing but static on any of the feeds until she'd cleared the building…guaranteed."

Ruby's wiry little body squeezed between them all until she was front and center. "Run it back please, Tristan." When he nodded, she laid her hand on his shoulder and whispered, "Such a nice young man." Jameson wanted to laugh, the older witch had done the same thing to him one afternoon when he'd been about to burst a vessel over something Kit had pulled. He wasn't sure what the spell was, but just the touch of her hand to his shoulder had calmed all the raging waters. Jameson watched as Tristan visibly relaxed and took what Jameson assumed was his first deep breath in hours.

"Kit is right, Carla never allows herself to be photographed. It isn't vanity as many assume." Looking from Jameson to Trev, she added, "She was always cautious, because putting your image out there for all to see when you are fighting the forces of evil is like handing your enemies a loaded weapon, but ever since the night your parents were killed, she has been meticulous—practically obsessive, about never being captured on film. She always feared being taken from Kit before her darling daughter was ready." Jameson saw Kit's eyes widen in surprise, he knew his lovely mate wasn't particularly close to her mother because his mother-in-law seemed to have impossibly high standards for her daughter. But now, he couldn't help but wonder if it hadn't all been about keeping Kit safe until she was ready to learn everything she'd need to fulfill her destiny. Ruby had talked to both he and Trev about the prophecy, so he knew the expectations others had for Kit were extremely high. Since Ruby had begun training Kit, Carla seemed to have mellowed, and now he had to wonder if he hadn't just been given a clue to that mystery.

"Well, someone wanted us to think it was your mother. But it seems odd that someone who knows her well enough to impersonate her isn't aware of her aversion to having her photograph taken." Jameson knew Tristan was essentially thinking out loud, it was the way his friend processed information, so he simply waited, then held his hand up when he thought Ruby was going to respond. "Unless, she's been seen at some of your witchy-woo parties and one of her peers has switched teams."

"Witchy-woo parties? What the hell is that about? Good Lord, no wonder your wife swears you live under a rock, Tristan. For Goddess sake, read something besides a tech manual, hell, watch a sit-com or two. You bore the teens of the pack by overriding the television's remote control and playing the damned science crap all day long anyway."

"Kitten, might want to tone it down a bit, his ears are turning crimson and starting to sizzle." Jameson gave her a little swat and smiled when she frowned up at him. "That's one, my love." He would give her a pass for sassing Tristan—once, but his little witch knew better than to frown at her Dom.

"Well, I didn't say his reasoning wasn't spot on. I simply took exception to the witchey woo comment, that was just plain sexist and insulting. I'll have you know, those witch gatherings are full-blown orgies with food served on naked bodies and drinks poured from floating goblets of gem-encrusted gold. Non-magicals beg to be included, and just last month I agreed to take Angie and Julie along next time." Jameson really was worried Tristan's head was going to spin around atop his shoulders.

"Really? When is the next one?" Braden's eyes were bright with anticipation and Jameson almost hated to watch as Kit burst his bubble. He had to give the kid credit, this time his timing was perfect. Braden's interest had distracted Tristan from playing right into Kit's hands.

"Of course not. Geez, Braden, think, my friend—would I have just told both of my mates that if it were true? Hell, they'd never let me go to one of the large coven conventions." Kit had emphasized her point by smacking the young wizard upside the head and shaking her head as if he were dim-witted.

"Unless of course you might be playing them by saying you were only playing them." This time Jameson was the one who smacked him, damned kid just didn't know when to quit.

"Knock it off you two. My mate is missing and you two are doing some sort of 'Who's on first' comedy routine. Focus, people." It was unusual for Nick Michaels to take a hard stance and everyone in the room froze for a couple of heartbeats before nodding. Tristan was ordinarily the more serious of the two brothers, so Nick's intensity spoke volumes about the level of anxiety permeating the room.

Jameson straightened to his full height and cleared his throat to re-center the attention to the front of the room. "Let's remember why we're here *and* why we're a good team. We all want to find Angie and we will because we'll use all available means to do so. But we're a strong team because we analyze information thoroughly. We each see the problem from a unique perspective and we approach things differently so we don't miss anything. And above all we remember safety is our number one priority."

Kit slipped her small hand inside his and squeezed in silent thanks before she stepped to the side where Nick stood. Giving him a quick hug, she said, "I'm sorry. We weren't trying to be disrespectful. I think it was just a release valve for some of our worry, but you were right to call it to a halt."

"My brother and I appreciate your help more than you know." He gave her a quick squeeze before turning her back to the screen, "Now, we need to figure out who might have been impersonating your mom so we can find our mate."

Ruby was already speaking on the phone and then turned the device toward the screen. When Jameson gave her a questioning look, she merely shrugged, "FaceTime. Braden helped me set it up. I'm witch-techy now, damn I wish Webster had lived long enough to know I made up a new word. He was a real stick in the mud you know."

Carla's exasperated voice sounded from the small screen, "For God's sake, mother, spare us the history lesson and run the tape." Everyone in the room laughed as Ruby shrugged and turned her phone back to the security monitor and Tristan restarted the short clip. Jameson couldn't help but smile when he heard his father-in-law's low whistle. Richard Harris was a powerful wizard but that fact was often overlooked because his personality was usually eclipsed by his much more out-going wife. Jameson respected Richard's quiet but methodical approach to problems and was anxious to hear his take of the video.

Carla's sharp tone brought Jameson's thoughts back to the problem at hand, "Oh my stars and garters, that does look like me. But you already know that, so let's get right to it. This sort of imitation requires a lot of concentration and focus, or perhaps help. Run it back a ways, I want to see who proceeds her and who follows."

After several minutes of expanding their search Carla's excited voice sounded, "Stop there. See? There she is."

This time it was Richard who answered, "Is that Twila? The young witch the Council asked you to mentor?"

"Yes it is. I don't know who was pretending to be me, but I know who was helping her and it gives us a starting point. Cecil, I'd say you have a serious mole problem."

"It would appear so, I do believe I'll give my fellow council members another call. And if they have time-zone issues—well, frankly Scarlet, I don't give a damn." Jameson laughed because he'd never met a group of people who could quote movie trivia like the magicals he'd encountered. When he'd asked Richard about it one evening over coffee, he'd explained that because they often lived for more than two hundred years witches and wizards had a lot more spare time. Richard had laughed as he'd recounted a rather colorful discussion he'd shared with Ivan Pavlov and Sigmund Freud where the two psychologists heatedly debated the reasons for, but not the fact that, creative minds are more open to mystical beliefs.

Richard had eventually lost Jameson in the discussion, but the bottom line had been clear—highly intelligent people were far more likely to accept the reality of things unseen. They understood and accepted there were powers at work around them that simply couldn't be explained away as coincidence. Jameson had seen the same phenomena play out himself when Kit's friend, Libby. The woman was quickly making a name for herself in both chemistry and neuroscience. She was currently a professor at NYU but Jameson and Trev hoped to change that in the near future. Libby's easy acceptance of what she'd found at the Wolf estate was a prime example of what Richard had been trying to point out. Libby was also another young professional woman who was burning the candle at both ends. For just a moment Jameson wondered if Charlie had made any progress with her, vowing to check in with him about it later, Jameson returned his attention to the conversation around him.

Jameson had always prided himself on being the type of leader who surrounded himself with good people and then stepped back, letting them do their jobs with as little interference as possible. As he watched those around him working together to make plans, he was grateful his fathers had consistently been incredible role models. They'd always explained their reasoning to both he and Trevlon so they understood all the minutia of leadership, not just how to boss people around. By the time the room began clearing out, everyone knew what they were supposed to do and they all seemed set on their tasks.

When Jameson shifted his attention to Kit, she was looking up at him expectantly. Shaking his head at her unasked question, he said, "Nothing for you just yet, kitten. Well, nothing aside from spending some quality time with your mates before you go." Running his fingers slowly down the side of her face until they slid under her hair to wrap around the back of her neck so he could pull her closer, he leaned down to speak softly against her ear, "Playroom. Strip. Kneel. Wait." Before he'd even released her Jameson could feel her trembling beneath his touch—and he knew his sweet mate well enough to know the reaction didn't have anything to do with fear. *Perfect.*

Chapter Three

Kit paced the long marble hallway listening to the sharp echo as the heels of her black leather boots collided with smooth stones that had welcomed visitors for several centuries. She marveled at the way the sound seemed to bounce between the polished rock walls, floor, and ceiling as if it was a calling card announcing her arrival. *Of course the ancients built their meeting place here, what better protection from outside evil than a crystal cave you lined with marble?* Granted the place was also truly spectacular—beautiful, ornate, and rich with history. The entire room was nearly luminescent despite the dim wall sconces providing limited amounts of light, but damn it was noisy. She was mentally reviewing what she planned to say and the best way for her to think was to keep moving. But the flipping noise was even starting to annoy her and she was the one causing it. When she looked up at her granny, Trev, and Braden, they all grinned at her. Trev walked to her and pulled her close, "Yes, it's quite annoying, baby, but if it helps you settle down we'll all just cope. We may be deaf or bat-shit crazy in the end, but we'll just have to wait and see about that part."

She appreciated his efforts to lighten her mood, and tried to smile in return but knew she'd failed miserably when he folded her into his arms and just held her against his chest. "You're going to do fine, baby. Surely they'll listen to reason and as long as you don't plan anything too outlandish, I can't imagine them arguing. After all, they seem keen on keeping Braden safe and Angie has been instrumental in his healing and happiness."

Trev hit upon a key point without even knowing it and Kit was struggling to block her thoughts from him. Blocking wasn't a skill she'd mastered yet, she doubted it would ever be something she managed easily. Trev's mentioning not doing anything outlandish was point-on because that was exactly what she had planned. The only way to resolve this quickly was to hit the enemy fast and hard, and the best way to do that was skate along the fine line between light and dark magic. What some might feel was colluding with the enemy, Kit viewed as using all of the resources available to her.

When Kit felt the muscles of Trev's chest stiffen against her cheek, she knew she hadn't been successful in blocking him, but just as he pulled back to speak the enormous door beside her opened and she was summoned inside. Stepping through massive wooden doors that hung on pounded iron hinges was like stepping back in time, and just before the door closed Trev's voice filled her mind and his fear for her filled her heart. "Don't. Baby. Please." Kit knew both of her mates were worried she would take unnecessary risks with her safety, but they were wrong. Oh, she intended to take a lot of chances if it became necessary, but necessary was the operative word.

Taking in the room she'd stepped into, Kit found herself temporarily frozen in her tracks. It was as if she'd been transported back a couple of centuries, her mind playing through scenes as if she'd seen them herself. The experience was unnerving, almost like watching a series of movies clips being projected in her mind. And in each of those clips, the room looked exactly as it did now, the only thing that changed was the faces of those around her.

The floors were polished white crystal that seemed to be drawing energy from the very air and shimmering with the effects. The horseshoe shaped table was exactly as she'd always pictured the round table of Camelot, save the opening for visitors to stand close without feeling as though they were actually a part of the Supreme Council's elite membership. The table sat on risers befitting the status of those seated around it, but in Kit's mind it was more about intimidation than respect. The witches and wizards who made up the Council were supposed to be elected based on skill, experience, life experiences, and the desire to serve the ranks from which they'd risen. But even as a young girl, Kit had noted that it seemed that by the time they'd made their way into such a position of power, they'd forgotten what it was like to be young and learning. She'd struggled to understand why she should revere the opinions of those who'd never once lived in the world as it is today. Many of the people seated in front of her hadn't lived in the *real world* in more than a century—how could they possibly understand the questions and challenges those under them were facing?

The room was lined with deep blue draperies with gold brocade that shimmered as it reflected the golden light from the wall sconces. The air was filled with a rich and woodsy incense that brought to mind the circles of light covens had been practicing in forests since the dawn of time. The entire room almost pulsed with the heartbeats of those who had proceeded her and Kit let the feelings wash over her, losing herself in the rich history. For the first time in her life, Kit was truly grateful for the gift of her magical heritage and she wanted to soak up every bit of the feeling she could before she was forced to face those who were watching her with amused interest.

When she saw Cecil's smile, Kit knew each member of the Council had been listening intently as her mind had wandered about untethered. Even though he'd been the one to catch her eye, he wasn't the first to speak. "Don't worry, it happens all the time. This whole set-up is pretty intimidating—intentionally for those who are here for certain reasons." The older man on her right spoke with just enough Irish brogue to make Kit smile, she'd always loved the way the people from the Emerald Isle spoke. "Aye, I grew up not far from the cottage your friend, Braden, described. I've always felt a particular interest in the young man, perhaps that's the reason. But, that isn't the reason you are here, is it?"

Kit nodded, hoping the gesture conveyed her respect as well as her agreement. "No it isn't. But thank you for your patience while I tried to take everything in. And you're right, it is intimidating, but it's also magnificent." She paused, letting her gaze taken in each of the witches and wizards sitting in front of her, "I've come to ask permission to use every resource available to me to bring Angie Wolf-Michaels home safely." Kit didn't see any reason to waste the Council's time, plus she was more than anxious to find Angie and return her to her mates.

Several of the Council members raised their brows, but Cecil was the one who spoke, "Kit, perhaps you need to clarify *any means necessary* since all of us are aware that you're still training."

"Yes, and the temptation to step over the line is even more powerful when you are new." The wizard who had spoken the words smiled, but his eyes were filled with concern.

"And you have an emotional stake in this if I'm not mistaken." Kit nodded at the witch who had made the comment. The woman was stunning, Kit had no idea how old the woman was, but she hoped she would age as beautifully as the witch who was now blushing a lovely pink. "Thank you, my dear. I assure you beauty is a double edged sword as I'm sure you already know." Kit smiled in return and nodded, because she did indeed know what it was like to be judged on her appearance and not her mind.

Kit couldn't argue with anything they'd said. Each Council member who had spoken had raised legitimate concerns—her only hope was to assure them she had a strong enough sense of right and wrong to avoid the pitfalls she knew others had fallen prey to. "You are all right. Each of you. But I assure you I'm not easily swayed and my sense of right and wrong was firmly in place long my training started. I'm not willing to sell my soul to Damian. We all know he is seeking an alliance, not to possess me. He needs both Braden and I in order to gain the type of power he seeks. Damian is not a fool, he knows I'm more powerful than he is—I've already proven that."

Cecil leaned back in his chair twirling a fountain pen so quickly between his slender fingers Kit worried ink was going to start flying everywhere. He studied her for so long, she had to fight the urge to fidget. He finally leaned forward and asked, "Are you willing to take Ruby with you? Absent that, we'd have to find another mentor and that would take time. And I'm worried for the young shifter's safety already. She's an amazing physician and there are great things in her future—she's destined to make remarkable contributions to the care of children. She and your friend, Libby, are going to be quite famous—well, assuming we get her back quickly."

"Agreed. These sort of things tend to derail people from the path their souls outlined on the other side." This comment from the youngest member of the group, a woman who looked so tiny Kit wondered if she was sitting on a booster seat. Her purple robe shimmered like silk and stood out from the more sedate robes the other members wore. When she smiled at Kit, the warmth it inspired was almost a physical reaction. *How odd. It felt like she wrapped me in a warm breeze.* At that thought, the woman merely nodded. The young witch's magic left Kit feeling as though she'd been hugged by a long lost friend—it was both comforting and unsettling in its familiarity.

Turning her attention back to Cecil, she noticed his lips quirked in a knowing smile. "Yes, sir. I am more than willing to take my grandmother along, but I want to be the lead on this. I'm not willing to take chances with her safety and I'm worried her reactions aren't as quick as they once were."

Most of the members chuckled softly and the man sitting next to Cecil shook his head, "Heed my advice, young woman, and don't let Ruby hear you say that."

"Too late, Bart." Kit was surprised to see her mother and grandmother both standing behind her. When Granny Good Witch turned to Kit she was frowning, "And you, my sweet granddaughter, better watch yourself. I'll show you slow reactions. Why that's just plain insulting. We'll see who is faster, just you wait. I'll let you lead this, but we're going to have a serious discussion about you thinking I'm ready for the old witches' home. As if."

Well fuck a duck in a big yellow truck, that's all I need, a pissed off granny.

Her grandmother moved into the center of the circle and Kit watched as the air around her began to shimmer.

The sparkling light was the most brilliant combination of colors imaginable, and seeing her grandfather's image emerge filled Kit's heart with joy. He turned and winked at her before turning back to the Council. She stepped closer hoping to hear what they were discussing, only to discover they were speaking in Latin. *Well, that's just plain rude. What the hell is that about?* Her mother leaned down and spoke softly against her ear, "Drama—well, they are going to claim it is tradition, which is technically true. But if you ask me, you grandfather is providing some insight that may help or hinder you, and he doesn't want to prejudice you."

"Want to run that by me again?" Kit had refrained from rolling her eyes at her mother's obtuse remark, but just barely. Carla Harris was incredibly bright and an extremely powerful witch, but both of those things also made her very difficult to understand at times. Oh, she thought she was being clear and was often completely befuddled when others didn't agree.

He mother's sigh let Kit know she wasn't impressed with the question, but she explained anyway. "He's gotten the scoop and he'd filling them in. Damn, my Latin is too rusty for me to keep up and I doubt Mother will share everything she knows. They'll use this as a test of sorts for you. They believe you are the one mentioned in the prophecy, but they want to be sure. But I don't want them to sacrifice Angie just to test their theory."

"What?" The question had come out far louder than she'd intended and when all eyes turned to her, all she could do was shrug and apologize.

"Good Goddess, keep your voice down. You're already pushing your luck just being here. And you better hope this wraps up quickly because your *mate* is faunching at the bit outside the door. Anyway, what I was trying to explain is that no one here sees this as the crises you do." When Kit gasped, her mother let out an exasperated sigh. "It isn't that they don't think Angie is important, it's just that we are fairly certain where she'd being held, the real question is what is it going to take to get her back without losing you in the process—something that is completely off the table by the way."

Kit wanted to argue, but knew it would just be an exercise in frustration. Her mother was rarely wrong about anything involving the magical community. Carla Harris had always been deeply committed to promoting the status of witches and more often than not she was a mediator when things went to hell between different groups. When Kit looked back to where her grandmother stood, she could see the lines of frustration bracketing her mouth. Ruby Stone wasn't happy about something and whatever had set her off was clearly a problem for her grandfather as well because even though his image was fading quickly, Kit could see him cross his arms over his chest as he shook his head.

By the time Kit had listened quietly as the Council handed down their decision and she'd walked out of their chambers, she was practically vibrating she was so angry. *How could they be so callous about Angie's safety? Doesn't her life mean anything to them?* It seemed to Kit that they had been far more worried about identifying the traitor who had managed to slip past their security to intern within their hallowed halls more than they were about the life of a young woman they were leaving hanging in the balance. Hell, if she followed all the guidelines they'd given her, she wouldn't have a prayer of rescuing her friend. *Document each step planned in detail and forward written copies to each member prior to acting?* If there had ever been a rule made to be broken, it was that one. In Kit's view the entire trip had been a wash, and the instant they stepped out into the cool night air the rage she'd been holding back burst to the surface. When she stretched her arms out wide lightning snapped from her fingers illuminating the night. Turning her face up to the sky, Kit felt the moonlight burst through the rolling clouds and shine down on her. It was as if the heavens had decided to endorse her anger by shining nature's spotlight on her from above. She shouted, "Devin, I am coming for you. Save yourself and return Angie to her home or turn her over to me."

Kit hadn't really expected him to hear her. Her plea to the dark sky had been more about venting than actually trying to contact Damian's brother. But one of the things they'd discovered about her magic was that it was amplified by anger and fear. No one knew exactly how or why—but there wasn't any doubt that was the case. Her granny stood aside watching as Kit tried to pull the calm of nature to herself, but the only thing that had helped was Trev's touch. Since shifters were earthbound creatures, both Trev and Jameson acted as lightning rods for Kit. When she was overwhelmed by the energy that rolled over her when her emotions took over, their touch was often enough to dispel the worst of the excess.

During a discussion while traveling to meet with the Council, Ruby had explained, that in fact, it was Kit's inability to moderate the energy she attracted that was one of the Council's chief concerns. They feared she could easily fall prey to the lure of dark magic partly because of it would appear that she was more in control, at least in the beginning. Kit had felt it was an unjust argument because strong emotions would fuel reactions in anyone. But her granny had disagreed, shaking her head and explaining,

"That's just it, Kit, power must equate to responsibility *and* control at all times, or its use is always going to be questioned." Kit hadn't fully understood the truth of that statement until this moment, but even then she didn't have long to consider all the implications because Devin's voice filled her mind.

'The queen's blood runs true in your veins, meet me tomorrow where she lies cold and still. Bring Braden but no one else or your sharp-tongued friend loses what little favor still remains. Tomorrow. Sunset.'

Chapter Four

Trevlon Wolf paced the length of the luxury suite, cell phone in hand listening to his brother list all the reasons their mate should not be allowed to meet with Devin alone. Jameson hadn't mentioned one assertion Trev hadn't already used in his numerous discussions with Kit—and not one of the very persuasive arguments had met with even a sliver of success. But right now Trev's problem was calming his brother down enough to actually find a workable solution to the problem. *Honestly, sometimes I'm not sure which of us is the most stubborn.* "I heard that, and it's our mate. I'm right, so it's simply tenacity. Kit is wrong, so she is being stubborn."

"Yeah, well thanks for clearing that up, but playing semantics games isn't going to solve this problem, now is it?" *Fuck it*, nothing he'd said had seemed to make any difference to her. Trev knew his brother could use his compelling voice to demand her compliance, but neither of them relished that idea. There were a lot of reasons they were both reluctant to go to that extreme, it was a perk of being the pack Alpha that Jameson used rarely. Once a command was spoken with the compelling voice, there was absolutely no question—it would be followed, but the recipient often resented their free will being bypassed, and both Jameson and Trevlon understood the inherent problems that caused.

He could hear his twin's sigh of frustration and knew from experience Jameson was running his free hand through his dark hair. They were not only identical twins, but also virtually mirror images of one another, and more often than not, they felt one another's emotions. They had always looked so much alike there were actually only a couple of people who had never mistaken them one for the other. Kit hadn't understood how anyone *could* confuse them—and that meant more to both he and Jameson than it probably should.

"I don't want to compel her. She'll resent it and I'm not sure I'd blame her. The message we'd be sending to not only our mate, but to our entire pack, would be that we don't trust her to do what we know she is here to do. Damn, this is exactly the sort of thing that defines her destiny. How can we deny her this?" Jameson's voice was heavy with regret and worry, and Trev fully understood Jameson's dilemma. Even though they were both considered pack Alphas, as the first-born, Jameson was the more senior leader and he always tried to shoulder the worst of the burden alone.

As they ended the call, Trev turned to see Kit standing in the doorway, her eyes shining with unshed tears. He held his arms open and she stepped quickly into his embrace. "Talk to me, baby."

"It's you...well, both of you. Your faith in me fills my heart with gratitude. I know that it's killing you to let me do this—but you're not going to stop me because it's what I *need* to do. I know I haven't known Angie as long as you have and we are not blood relatives. But she is still my family in all the ways that matter—and she needs my help." Trev was humbled by his sweet mate's words, even though he was worried she was giving he and Jameson far too much credit. Rather than saying anything that might cause her further upset, he simply held her. She certainly didn't need any added distraction before leaving to meet Devin.

🐾 🐾 🐾

KIT AND BRADEN rode in silence to the open field where Aradia was said to have been buried. There was no marker per the Queen of Witches request, she'd known her gravesite would become a contentious memorial and she'd been adamantly opposed to that idea. Fearing future persecution of those who would follow, the wise witch had demanded the exact location of her grave never be revealed. From everything Kit had read about the woman considered the Queen of Witches, she'd been a firm believer in living for the future rather than in the past. Every witch's Book of Shadows contained bits of wisdom attributed to Aradia that had been passed down generation to generation for countless centuries. Kit's favorite was the reminder to never be humbled so much that you stumbled over our own past.

As they exited the small rental car, Braden looked over at her and winked, "Remember, individually we are good, but together we are superheroes. And Granny Good Witch promised me a cape when we get Angie back." When she cast him a sidelong glance, he chuckled, "What? I know I can't fly with a cape, but it will be fun to mess with the kids back at the estate." She shook her head, in so many ways he was an adult, but there were still moments when the childhood he'd missed bubbled to the surface. Everyone at the estate relished those moments because to their minds it meant he was healing and maturing into the powerful wizard he was destined to become.

Braden's childhood had been cut far too short because he'd been the focus of Damian's obsession from the time the dark wizard learned the child was his grandson. Braden's father had run away with him after the young boy's mother was killed. For years, father and son had barely managed to stay one-step ahead of the man obsessed with the young boy, but their luck had finally run out and Braden lost his father, too.

As the sun started to sink beneath the horizon, a brilliant ball of orange light shimmered several feet in front of where Kit and Braden stood waiting. For several seconds the light simply hovered and spun slowly around and Kit wondered if it was ensuring they'd come alone. When Devin finally emerged as an ill-defined mist, he scanned the area before focusing on the two of them. Just as Kit opened her mouth to demand he give them proof Angie was still alive, she appeared next to him.

"What the hell is that?" Braden started to step forward as he spoke but Kit placed her hand on his shoulder to hold him back. Devin's posture had shifted immediately and Kit was worried about the young man's safety. Even though Angie appeared to be trapped in some sort of glass bubble, she appeared to be unharmed. Braden turned back to Devin and took a menacing step forward before Kit pulled him back once again. "Can she hear us?" Just then they saw Angie waving her arms and she looked as though she was shouting but they couldn't hear anything. "Well, guess that answers that question. Hey, how long can she stay in there without fresh air?" Kit wanted to roll her eyes, leave it to Braden to shift so quickly to logical and scientific observations. Good Goddess it was certainly easy to see he and Angie were related. Kit was far more worried that none of them were going to live long enough for oxygen to ever be an issue.

"Don't worry about the bubble. It is soundproof, but she will not come to any harm being in there. She had been treated well as I'm sure she will tell you, assuming you are willing to negotiate with me." Kit's interest was piqued because Devin had emphasized the word *me* and she found it odd that he'd make that distinction.

'What do you make of this, Kit? Why did he say we are negotiating with him? Do you think we were right the last time when we sensed his reluctance to be his brother's lackey?'

Kit appreciated the telepathic link she and Braden had established. They'd spent many hours practicing the silent method of communication and she was grateful they shared a way to speak without being heard. *'I was just thinking the same thing. Let's see where this takes us, shall we?'*

Returning her focus to Devin, Kit demanded, "Tell us what you want. Why would you want to kidnap Angie? And who was responsible?" Devin rolled his eyes at her questions and it quickly became clear to Kit that Devin wasn't particularly interested in discussing the details.

"I can't tell you everything—at least not yet, but you already know that. And I'm sure you have already figured out that my brother wants to trade the good doctor for his grandson." When she opened her mouth to speak he held up his hand in a silent gesture silencing her. "I already know that isn't going to happen and in truth I'd be somewhat disappointed in you if you agreed to such an exchange. Remember, I said your negotiations are with me, not my brother." For the first time in days, Kit felt some of the tension leave her body as the possibility that they might get Angie back without extreme violence loomed before her.

During the next half hour, Devin paced so quickly

along a line in front of them that he literally wore a path in the grass beneath his feet. There were times as he spoke that Kit wondered if he was still speaking to them or he'd simply become lost in his own thoughts. Devin outlined his brother's plan to take over the Supreme Council after he was freed from behind the sealed portal—and realizing how close Damian was to making it happened scared Kit more than she wanted to admit.

"Kit, the magic you used the night you sent Damian behind the seal was dark, very dark. And the remarkable thing is you were completely untrained. I know the powers that be are telling you they don't know how you managed it, but that isn't exactly true. They know it was dark magic, what they don't know is how you learned it. Whether it's innate knowledge or simply natural ability, then they have a really big problem on their hands."

"Explain why they consider it their problem." As much as Kit wanted to deny his words, she honestly wasn't sure she could. Something about his observation resonated in her soul as the truth though. She didn't like it, but she'd never been one to deny reality even if it didn't fit well with the way she wanted to see herself. Her passionate response to Jameson's dominance that first night at the club was a perfect example. As much as she had wanted to be outraged by his high-handed behavior, she hadn't been able to deny her body's intense response to his dominance.

"There is a battle coming, Kit, you already know this, but what may surprise you is how quickly the scales are tipping in Damian's favor." Devin ran his hand through his shaggy black hair in a gesture Kit recognized as pure frustration. "I've always been torn between my brothers. Damian is as dark as a moonless night, but he had always treated me well, at least until recently. He's losing touch with reality and that doesn't translate well to interpersonal communication and people skills. Marcus, on the other side, has always done what is right, but he is an ass—as I'm sure you have already noted." In Kit's opinion, that was an understatement. She'd been less than comfortable with Marcus from the beginning and nothing that had happened since then had done anything to change her mind.

"I understand what you have said and agree, but what's coming is not the issue at this moment. Getting Angie home safely is all I care about." *Well, that isn't exactly true, but no need to snatch the olive branch out of his hands and smack him over the head with it.*

His sly smile let Kit know her thoughts hadn't been as private as she intended them to be. Braden's word drifted into her mind lilting with warmth and laughter. *'Well, duh, Kit. You were fairly well mentally shouting, so there wasn't much chance he wouldn't hear you.'* The young wizard's words made her smile, he could be so impertinent at times that he, well—quite frankly he reminded her of herself at that age.

"Damian won't be pleased that you have managed to free the woman he considers his bargaining chip, but he will be impressed with my description of the dark magic you used to accomplish it." When he smiled, Kit realized this was the first time she'd seen him do it. The gesture totally transformed his appearance and he looked much younger and infinitely more approachable in that moment. But, the light left his eyes too quickly as he continued, "As to what I want in exchange—I want to help train you for the coming battle. I am no longer interested in aligning myself with Damian and I'm willing to help defeat him. His plans have escalated to the point the price is going to be far too high, and there are a lot of people who will pay with their lives." Kit knew there was more to it than that, but was certain he wasn't going to share the rest anytime soon.

Bringing him into the fold was dangerous on so many levels she was having trouble just tracking all the potential problems as they ran through her mind. And worst of all, Kit knew the guilt she felt when he'd known she'd been experimenting showed clearly in her expression and Braden laughed, "Damn, Kit, it isn't like it was a secret. You know Tristan and Nick don't miss anyone going in or out of the house, and your mates probably know every detail about your dreams they watch you so closely. How did you think everybody and their dogs didn't know where you were going? Geez." She managed to catch herself just before she gave him the "you roll your eyes at me again like that young lady and I'll roll them right out of your head" speech she'd gotten so often at that age. Of course she'd have to edit it a bit, but still, the idea of turning into her mother wasn't at all appealing. She'd heard enough of her friends talking over drinks to know it was a universal dilemma.

Sighing to herself, she turned back to Devin, "I will agree to work with you." *Because I'd do anything to get Angie back.* "But even you have to know what a difficult sell this is going to be. The Wolf Pack is going to be more than a little reluctant to believe your change of heart, even though they will be grateful for Angie's safe return. And the Supreme Council is probably going to want to send at least one overseer." Hell's bells and horseshoe nails, knowing that paranoid bunch, they'd send a whole contingent. And none of this was even considering the conniption fit her two mates were going to throw, just thinking about *that* conversation sent shivers up her spine.

Devin's sly smile let her know he'd already foreseen everything she'd mentioned. "I've arranged transportation for you since my brother's *guest* doesn't have a passport. Everything is made in Trevlon Wolf's name, he and your grandmother will be waiting for you at the private field. I've sent the directions to both of your mobile phones so you shouldn't have any trouble finding your way." All Kit could do was stare at Devin in open-mouthed shock. Was he for real? Who kidnapped a woman in hopes of joining forces with their family? Again, he must have known exactly where her mind had gone because she shook his head, "I am not the one who arranged for Dr. Michaels to be taken from the hospital. Personally, I think her work is far too important to risk her safety, but as I said, my brother isn't at all concerned about the future of anyone but himself. Angie will tell you the names of the women involved, but I'd be willing to bet you already have that information."

With a flick of his wrist the bubble around Angie vanished and she ran to Braden putting herself between the two wizards. Before Kit could respond Devin as gone, but his voice rang through her mind, *'I'll meet you in the meadow during the next full moon, your word is your bond, Kit—and I know you won't disappoint me. There is too much at stake, your children's future hangs in the balance. Little Ryan's and Adana's fates are in your hands.'*

Chapter Five

Kit looked around the dungeon and wondered how her husbands had managed to make so many upgrades to the large space without her noticing. Granted, she had been gone a few days, but Trev had been with her and the changes she noted in their private playroom definitely had his signature style. Everything was period perfect for the medieval era most commonly associated with dungeons and torture devices, and those things simply weren't important to Jameson. And even though the pieces of furniture filling the large stonewalled room might be designed for erotic pleasure, they were still intimidating. She wasn't sure she would ever be completely at ease with the harsher side of the lifestyle her two mates had enjoyed prior to their mating, but then again, they didn't seem particularly excited about her becoming *too comfortable* either.

She'd been lost in her thoughts, Kit hadn't realized they'd both stopped talking off to the side. *Oh fricking fairy farts, did they ask me something? They get really pissy if I don't stay focused on what's happening.* Keeping focused had never been one of Kit's strong points. Jameson's growl filled the air, "Kitten? Are you going to answer the question?" *Question? Shit, shit, shit. What the hell did they ask?*

"Umm, well, I must have missed it the first time…Sir." *Always a good idea to tack that on when in trouble.* The

Dominant portions of both of men's personalities seemed to respond well to her submissive side, but adding any additional *sucking up* verbiage was a real balancing game she rarely got exactly right.

"Indeed, I do believe you did, baby. Maybe if you'd try to stay in the moment, you might catch things easier." Trev's voice was deceptively gentle, but Kit wasn't fooled. On the surface he appeared to be the gentler of the two, but he was actually more of a stickler for protocol in the lifestyle than Jameson. Trev had been furious with her for agreeing to work with Devin from the moment she'd first explained the conditions she'd agreed to in order to free Angie. He hadn't been able to openly complain without giving the impression Angie hadn't been worth it and being caught between a rock and a hard place seemed to have added a lot of fuel to his fury.

Glancing over she met Jameson's heated gaze. They had already stripped her and secured her to the strangest St. Andrew's Cross she'd ever seen. The wooden beams of the cross narrowed so they were almost non-existent in the middle, and the end-points were aligned with tracks that Kit assumed allowed the cross to be tilted and rotated in several different directions. The wide bands securing her were softly woven to prevent unnecessary pressure at any point and the Velcro tear away sections were strategically placed to allow access to every part of her trembling body. It was the only piece of equipment they'd added then made no attempt to hide the fact it was state of the art technology for kinksters. Just thinking about the ad they'd probably seen in *Torture Equipment Monthly* made Kit smile.

"Care to share what that thought was, kitten?" Jameson's voice sounded from right in front of her. *Holy hell how had he moved so close without her noticing?* When she gasped in surprise, he shook his head, "Kitten, I could have sprouted wings and flown around the room and you wouldn't have noticed. Now, stop stalling and tell us what you were thinking that made you smile."

"Oh, well, I was just admiring the new additions to the playroom, and I wondered about your...umm, sources for such novelties." Kit added her most sincere expression, but wasn't surprised when her blatant attempt to distract them didn't work.

"And? Don't insult us by editing, my love—we know you far too well." Oh brother and wasn't that the truth. Kit really believed they knew her better than she knew herself in a lot of ways.

"Well, I sort of thought maybe there was a catalog or something." They both just kept watching her, their postures mirror images of one another, their legs spread shoulder width apart and bulging biceps crossed over heavily muscled chests. Looking at them dressed in nothing but low-slung, faded jeans with their bare feet topped by the time worn fringes of hems dragging over the stone floor. Kit realized too late that she was staring and licking her lips in anticipation. "Okay, okay. I figure you probably get *Torture Equipment Monthly*, you know, sort of like *Consumer Reports*, but for kinky stuff." Geez, now that they'd forced her to say it out loud it didn't sound funny at all, talk about ruining a perfectly good joke.

Surprised by Trev's snort of laughter and Jameson's grin, Kit tried to shrug but they'd secured her so well she couldn't even lift her shoulder. Realizing she was well and truly at their mercy sent a zing of arousal straight to her sex and she knew neither of her mates had missed her scent when their nostrils flared. "We're going to remind you who you belong to, baby. You've made a bargain with a man who could hurt you and we take your safety very seriously. And even though you agreed to meet him away from the house in a feeble attempt to keep everyone else safe, you still agreed to work with him without any apparent consideration for your own well-being. And agreeing to meet him in a secluded place? Don't even get me started on all the reasons that fact earns you punishment. But the biggest problem is that you didn't consult either of us before you made this bargain." *Was he serious? Without consulting them? What the hell?* She was a grown woman who made her own decisions. Granted they were both her Alphas as well as her mates, but still—just the thought of having to get their approval to agree to training—not to mention that of everybody and their pup in the magical community was going to have their nose up in her business, well, that was just over the top. Hell, they knew all of it would be supervised to the nth degree so their comments grated on her last nerve.

"I'm not sure, brother, but I think perhaps you've touched upon a sticking point for our lovely subbie and mate. She sure seems to be taking her time processing that, don't you think?" Trev's teasing tone earned him a glare and when she saw his jaw tighten, Kit knew the scathing look she'd given him had been a huge error.

🐾 🐾 🐾

TREVLON WOLF HONESTLY believed he'd been more than patient with Kit. He'd nearly gone out of his mind with worry while she'd met with the Supreme Council. The enormous doors that closed between them had obviously been made of something very special or perhaps the wizards inside had put some sort of spell on them, because

Kit's thoughts had been completely blocked from him from the moment they'd locked together. It was if his mate had simply ceased to exist. The emptiness that had filled his soul had knocked him to his knees and had nearly driven him to distraction. Trev had suddenly understood why shifters who lose their mates die shortly thereafter. And then, when she and Braden had gone to meet Devin alone, he'd been even more crazed. It wasn't that he didn't have faith in her abilities, it was simply that he was terrified there would be a split second when she was distracted and that would be all the time an enemy needed to steal her from him forever.

When a messenger arrived instructing both he and Ruby to meet Kit and Braden at a private landing strip, he'd worried they were all walking into a trap. Ruby had assured him she wasn't picking up any negative trace magic, but not being able to confirm the safety of the situation himself had left him more than a little unnerved. But the worst had come after they'd all returned home and Kit had explained the conditions she'd agreed to in exchange for Angie's release. When he'd looked over at Jameson, Trev had actually wondered whether his brother's head was going to spin around on his shoulders or explode first.

They'd immediately begun planning a session in their newly remodeled dungeon as a way to release some of their stress as much as a way to remind their darling mate who she belonged to. But now, her continued defiance had just changed the game. She wanted to use those lovely eyes to look at them as if they were cretins? Well, they'd just rob her of that opportunity. Stalking over to the large armoire, Trev returned with a long, black silk scarf. "Baby, those glares have just tipped the scales, and not in your favor. Let's see if we can't make sure you don't dig yourself any deeper, shall we?"

Trev and Jameson both knew how independent Kit was—submission wasn't ever going to be easy for her, even though she embraced it with everything she was once they got her focused on what she was *feeling*. The biggest hurdle Kit faced in their D/s relationship was that her mind rarely shut down without their help. During a post-orgasmic haze once early in their relationship, she'd admitted the relief of not having to *think* was almost overwhelming though the glare she'd given him earlier made him doubt his feisty lover would admit that now. Her eyes blazed with anger as he slid the silk over them. When she opened her mouth to speak, he leaned forward and whispered against her ear, "Be very careful, baby, or you'll find yourself *gagged* as well." The low growl deep in her throat made Trev smile. For a shifter who'd never changed until they'd mated, she had certainly taken quickly to snarling.

'She seems less than impressed with your warning, brother. What do you say we give her reason to reconsider her surliness?'

'I completely agree, I'll clamp those beautiful nipples while you begin flogging her.' Trev pulled the first clamp from his pocket as he leaned down and covered the pink peak with his mouth. He loved blowing air over the damp skin and watching it draw up seeking his attention. He grazed his teeth over the tip clamping down gently before pulling back and letting it stretch even tighter before releasing it. Watching her breast jiggle, he fought the urge to press the mounds together and slide his cock between them and mark her chest with his seed. *'It's amazing how quickly that growl turns to a moan of pleasure, isn't it, baby?'* He loved being able to push his words into her mind, knowing they would resonate clear to her soul.

"Yes, ohhh, that feels so—argh!" Trev knew the moment the strands of the flogger thudded against her ivory skin just by her reaction. Feeling her tremble and her skin heat beneath his lips was nothing compared to the scent of her sweet honey. By the time they were finally ready to take her, Kit's sweet cream would be running in rivulets down the inside of her thighs. He and Jameson were both thrilled that she was always ready for them. Her body responded by preparing itself even when her mind was still playing catch-up.

Closing his teeth gently, he pulled back again and again until the peak was a sharp point begging for the jeweled clamp in his hand. Releasing the clamp over the tip and then tightening it until Kit hissed, he backed off the tension just a bit and grinned over her shoulder at Jameson. His brother was absorbed in his task and Trev was quickly becoming intoxicated by the smell of his mate's arousal. He couldn't wait to kneel in front of her and run his tongue over her pussy lips, tasting her need was intoxicating.

Lavishing his attention on Kit's other nipple, Trev felt her body shudder as she drew close to release, he pulled back to say, "Don't you dare come without permission, baby. That will buy you more trouble than you can take right now." Her sweet pleading fell on deaf ears. Neither he nor Jameson were in forgiving moods—at least not just yet.

"You had better listen to him, kitten. He is trying to save your ass—literally."

"I will try, but it…feels so deliciously wicked I'm not sure how long I can—hold out." Trev couldn't hold back his chuckle because they all three knew she would only be able to hold back as long as they allowed it. Either of them could push her over whenever they decided to, they knew her body's limits far better than she did at this point. There wasn't an inch they hadn't tasted, not a single place they hadn't kissed. The two of them had mentally mapped each one hot spot and catalogued her reactions. They'd routinely exploited the information without a shred of remorse.

Kit's soft panting brought Trev's mind back to the moment, with his hands over her shoulders, he could feel her muscles tighten in anticipation of the second clamp and he intended to make certain the intensity pushed her even closer to the edge. They were going to torture her with pleasure for as long as possible before any of them went over the edge.

"Let's see how you do with a bit of added weight, shall we, baby? I think these emeralds are going to look lovely against your creamy skin." When she gasped and jerked against the restraints, he smiled, "Oh, and did I mention that they are quite large. They're a gift from us to you. The stones have been in our family for hundreds of years, made into various configurations and pieces over the years, but I do believe our favorite jeweler has outdone himself this time." Watching the deep green stones sparkle as they caught the light from the wall sconces, Trev couldn't help but marvel at the way the soft light danced over the surface of the faceted stones.

'You'd better kick things up a notch, Jameson, she isn't going to last much longer—and neither am I. Her cream is already running in glimmering streams down the inside of her thighs.' Slowly he pressed butterfly kisses down her torso circling her naval with his tongue before pressing it inside to mimic what he planned to do when he reached her sweet pussy.

'Let's tilt her world a little bit. It'll bring her back from the edge and I'll distract her with one of the toys in my pocket. Let's see how she does with the clit clip.'

'Perfect. And then see if giving her something to wrap those

sweet lips around won't keep her out of trouble. If she can't speak maybe she won't be as apt to turn this into a punishment session rather than the pleasurable reminder we'd envisioned.' Trev pulled the small remote from the pocket of his jeans. When Kit felt the cross begin to move, she gasped in surprise. Reaching beneath her to palm the cheeks of her ass, Trev noticed how hot her skin felt against his palm—his brother had no doubt done a superb job of warming her up.

Leaning down, Trev used his lips to push the hood back before sucking her clit ruthlessly over the tops of his teeth. Kit screamed and Trev used the flat of his hand to give her sensitized ass a stinging swat. "This pink pearl is mine to decorate, baby. I'm going to put a lovely ring around it and leave it exposed for our pleasure." What she didn't know was that even the slightest movement of air over the exposed bundle of nerves was going to feel like a lover's caress. She was already so close, Trev wondered if he'd get the small device in place before she lost control.

🐾 🐾 🐾

JAMESON'S EMOTIONS WERE at war. A part of him wanted to paddle Kit's ass until she needed a pillow to sit on for the next several days. But another part wanted to fuck her senseless—sinking so deep in her that she'd never forget who she belonged to, and she'd never even consider putting herself in this sort of danger again. He'd stripped while Trev repositioned their new St. Andrew's Cross, Kit's face was now at the perfect height for him to slide his engorged cock past her sweet lips, but first he wanted to reconnect their spirits. For the first time since she'd walked into the club, he'd been forced to spend several nights away from her and he'd missed her with every beat of his heart. If something happened to her, Jameson wasn't entirely sure he'd survive.

Stroking a knuckle along the side of her face, he soothed her when she startled, "It's just me, kitten." His ego swelled when she tried to push her cheek against his hand. She was so much like the kitten he called her, seeking the warmth of his touch. "Your new jewelry looks beautiful laying against your creamy skin, my love. I'm going to enjoy playing with those lovely green jewels as I'm sliding over those ruby lips. And even though I can't see your eyes, I know these emeralds are the exact same color, but we'll check that later—when I remove them I want to see your eyes widen as your mind tries to distinguish the pleasure from the pain."

Jameson kept stroking the back of his finger slowly up and down the side of her neck, watching goose bumps race over her skin under his light touch. He was determined to draw this out despite the fact it was taking everything he had to keep from pushing clear to the back of her throat, sinking deep into her warm mouth. "You see, my love, this is all about reminding you that you belong to us. We don't expect you to seek our approval for everything you do. You are a brilliantly talented woman who has proven time and again how capable you are. But when you make choices that leave your wellbeing hanging in the balance, we'll expect you to confer with us beforehand. We'd expect the same consideration from any other member of the pack."

Jameson waited for a few seconds letting Kit's mind process his words before continuing. He could feel her struggle to stay focused on what he was saying when they were bombarding her senses. They'd learned that first night Kit's ability to multitask was amazing and that pushing her past that point wasn't easy. He wanted her to stop thinking and simply feel the power of their love for her. The connection between them was strong, but Jameson knew it would fade over time unless he and Trev continually reminded her how deeply their souls were linked.

"Your safety and happiness, and that of Ryan and Adana, are what we are here for—everything we do, we do for our family." Truer words had never left Jameson's lips. Using one hand to turn her mouth so he could rub the tip of his cock over her lips glazing them with the pearly pre-cum that had beaded at the end in anticipation, he hissed when she used her tongue to delve into the sensitive slit.

They had placed more than a hundred unlit candles around the room while preparing for their scene. Their mate's magic was a powerful force and was fed by emotion, the more aroused Kit became—the more she "let go", the more erratic her magic became. They'd discovered early on that giving Kit's magic a safe outlet—such as setting candlewicks aflame, was far safer than letting it find its own outlet. They had burned several sets of draperies and too many clothing items to count before making sure they always had plenty of candles on hand. As she sucked him deeper, Jameson's eyes closed and his head fell back, he groaned, "Fuck that feels so good. Knowing you are tasting me, that I'm surrounded by your sweet lips—hell, the heat of your mouth is almost too much." If he didn't watch out, she was going to steal his control and that wasn't what tonight was about.

The thought had no sooner moved through his mind than he heard Trev's soft laughter. *'Yeah, you had better be careful or she's going to own this scene and the two of us are going to end up looking like her subs instead of the other way around. I swear the woman's strongest magic is the way she draws us in.'*

'True, but holy fucking hell, her devil-blessed mouth is pure heaven. I just want to sink deep and shoot down her throat as you do the same with her pussy. If we fill her from both ends, perhaps she'll remember who this lovely body belongs to.'
Jameson had barely opened his eyes when the little minx redoubled her efforts and he felt fire begin to boil in his balls, threatening to burn a hole through his restraint and erupt any second.

"Oh no, kitten, you are not in control here. You are not going to tempt me over the edge, my control is stronger than that." Jameson spoke the words despite the fact he wasn't entirely convinced they were true. *'Fuck me, the minx can unravel me faster than I can fight it off. You had better step up your game, brother, or this is going to end far too soon.'*

Jameson and Trevlon Wolf had shared women for years. Their reputations as always being solidly in control of their orgasms were stellar. Hell, they'd been highly sought after Doms because they never came before the sub they were topping had come at least twice. They had been sexually active since high school—much to their parents' displeasure, and he'd never fought so hard to control himself. His connection to Kit was so strong he felt not only his and Trev's pleasure, but hers as well, and it pushed him further than he ever thought possible. Even Trev slapping his palm against her sex hadn't broken her resolve—Kit was determined and his body was happy to let her give him pleasure.

Looking down and watching his cock sliding in and out of Kit's mouth, knowing he was going to shoot his seed down her throat, marking her from the inside out, sent a flash of fire up his spine to set off fireworks in his brain and then shoot back down and out the end of his cock in flaming pulses he couldn't have held back if his life had depended upon it. Kit swallowed every drop he'd given her and for several seconds Jameson wasn't sure he was capable of forming a coherent word, let alone tell her how incredible she'd been.

Chapter Six

Kit's entire body felt like it was aflame. The blindfold might be blocking her vision, but the loss of that sense only served to enhance the others, and she could already smell the sage and citrus scent of the candles her magic was lighting. Her mind might battle her mates' dominance, but her body was completely enslaved to the two of them. She'd tried to run that night at the club, but Jameson Wolf had been ahead of her at every turn. By the time Jameson had gotten her upstairs into their office, she'd known it had already been too late to escape her fate.

Jameson's voice and his confidence had wreaked havoc with her resistance, but his scent was what had undone her. The minute she'd been close enough to get the full effect of his woodsy scent it had wrapped itself around her tying them together as securely as if he'd been using rope. By the time Trev made his way to their office Kit had already been drowning in desire despite what she had tried to tell them. From their first touch, both of her mates had been able to play her body like a finely tuned instrument.

Tasting the first drops of Jameson's pre-cum coating the tip of her tongue was ratcheting up her arousal exponentially. Kit was tired of waiting for him to push in further, but when she tried to suck him in deeper he'd initially pulled back trying to regain control. She'd known he was holding on by a thread and she felt her brain fog as she focused in on his pleasure. After he'd come, his release shooting against the back of her throat, Kit felt his emotions wash over her like a tidal wave of pure pleasure.

Within seconds he'd recovered and she was astonished when she realized his cock was still rigid against her tongue. She knew they both thought she had been trying to steal the reigns, but she really only wanted to feel the power that filled her when she brought them pleasure. *'And that isn't trying to take control, kitten?'* Damn and double damn it all to Dalmatians. When would she ever learn to monitor or shield her thoughts? And as much as she hated to admit it, he had a point—and didn't that just suck. Good Goddess it was annoying that they were almost always right. Sure, they had years of experience as sexual Dominants and Alphas, but it still frustrated her that she always seemed to be playing catch-up. Hell, there were days when she missed how simple her life had been before she'd found her mates.

"See? There she goes again. Her mind is a million miles away. We really need to work on keeping her *in the moment.* Let's see if this helps pull her back." Trev had barely gotten the words out when the palm of his handed slapped firmly against her sex. It wasn't a harsh blow, but it hadn't been expected either and Kit felt her entire body strain against the restraints as it tried to arch seeking more of the pleasure. "See how quickly it brings your body and mind back together, baby? It's remarkable how your body reacts, isn't it? Even when your mind tries to control things, it struggles to separate the pleasure from the pain when you are so aroused. I know you don't particularly *want* to see yourself as submissive but, baby, your body doesn't understand semantics, it understands what it craves."

Damn it all to the seventh level hell, stop psychoanalyzing everything and just get the fuck on with it already. The next slap to her sex was harsher but not as unexpected and pushed her perilously close to release. Kit's mind was already starting to fragment from the sensations bombarding her and holding back her orgasm was getting harder and harder with each breath she took. Tasting Jameson and marveling at how quickly he'd fully recovered, she wanted simply to lose herself as he slid over her tongue. The tangy, outdoorsy scent that was unique to him sent a fresh rush of moisture to her pussy. "Oh, baby, that is so hot. Watching your pussy cream for us is a turn on of the first order. Fuck me, I could watch the lips of your rose-colored sex flower open forever, but right now I want to sink balls deep and lose my mind in pleasure of your body." One quick thrust and he was fully seated inside her and Kit gasped at the sudden intrusion. The delicious stretch of her sensitive tissues set her entire body on fire.

"Suck me deep, kitten. I want to pull back from your mouth and see my cock slick with your sweet saliva and my come. I want to feel you sucking hard as if you are trying to suck another load of cum straight from my root. Feeling the tip bump against the back of your throat is the second best feeling in the world." *Second best? Excuse me, what the hell does that mean?* Jameson's soft groan of pleasure was followed by a chuckle, "It means the best feeling in the world is when your sweet pussy clamps down around my cock in a pulsing grip that milks the last drops from my body and splashes them against your womb. Knowing I'm shooting my seed deep inside my mate fulfills a part of me that reflects centuries of mating rituals enjoyed by my ancestors and are now imprinted on my soul."

Kit heard the words, and even in her lust-fogged state

she understood the depths of emotion that had accompanied them. One of the things she loved the most about her mates was their willingness to be emotionally open with her. They'd never attempted to hold back their feelings, and it had taken her a while to understand how valuable that gift truly was. They understood the emotional vulnerability of submission and their respect for that gift was returned tenfold in their own willingness to share exactly how they felt.

During a margarita fueled girls' night not long after she'd mated, her friend, Libby, had scolded her for not appreciating how lucky she was, and her mouthy friend's words had stung, but they'd been too true at the time. As Libby had so bluntly pointed out, one of the most remarkable things about shifters is their honesty. Just like the animals that make up a large part of their personalities, they are usually able to state their feelings without much consideration for modesty or fear of rejection. If you don't like what they have to say, you are welcome to move along—a trait free-speaking spirits like Libby appreciated to their very souls.

"Kitten, we know your heart was in the right place when you made the promise. Getting Angie home safely without a battle was perfect. But your insistence on following through is what we find problematic. You don't have to keep your word when dealing with those working with the dark side." Kit groaned at the loss because Jameson had pulled back from her to speak the words. In her heart she knew he was right, but there was something speaking to her that said he had important information and that he was truly tired of dealing with his brother. And if she was right, the entire magical community stood to gain tremendously from anything she might learn.

"But right now all I want to think about is how amazing your mouth feels as I slide my cock in and out of its warmth. I'm going to lose my mind again because your tongue will wrap itself around me, hugging my dick and pressing my length tightly against the ridges lining the roof of your mouth. And I want to watch your body accept the most intimate gift a man can give his mate as my brother shoots his seed deep into your womb." Kit groaned as both men set a thundering pace that sent her body into a freefall over the edge of mindless pleasure. The lightning strike of bliss scorched her very soul and Kit couldn't have held back her mind-bending need release even if her life had depended on it. She felt the blindfold being pulled away and then her mind barely registered Jameson's command to let go before her entire body shuddered as everything around her exploded in a wash of brilliant white light. So bright she saw it through her closed eyes and the entire room was still shimmering when she finally managed to open her eyes long seconds later.

When had they moved her to the bed? Moving her arm slowly between the soft sheets, Kit enjoyed the feel of the cool fabric as it slid unimpeded over her bare skin. She'd never experienced a release as soul shattering as the one Jameson and Trev had just given her, and Kit felt an unfamiliar unease move through her. Being a submissive and magical had often caused her to feel pulled in two directions. But this time the entire experience had been much more intense because of the power issues involved and her internal conflict was exponentially worse as a result.

Kit wasn't fooled, she knew her mates had been restaking their claim during the scene—she also understood that it had been more about reassuring themselves than reminding her. Her unease stemmed from the fact she'd been so lost in the moment she had so completely surrendered to them that she'd actually blanked out the last few minutes. As a magical, she had an inherent responsibility to maintain control of her emotions and reactions at all times. Losing control was dangerous for anyone with magical abilities, but it was particularly dangerous for someone with the level of natural ability Kit had shown herself to possess.

Granny Good Witch had been lecturing her for months about how critical it was to consistently maintain her self-control. Juggling these two very different aspects of her life was taking a toll on her—she just didn't know what to do about it. Clearly she hadn't done a very good job this evening because they'd released her from her restraints and moved her to the bed without her being aware of it, and that wasn't even mentioning all the candles she could see flickering all around the room. How was she ever going to make this work? How was she every going to juggle two such divergent aspects of her life forever? The struggle would just get harder as her skills increased. At times like this she really missed her old life—it had been so much less complicated. Her only real goal had been avoiding mating. She'd gone to great lengths to steer clear of any place she thought there was even a remote chance she'd encounter her future mate. *Damn Libby and her sweet little elfin face and persuasive nature. If I hadn't gone with her dancing that night...*

When her brain finally came fully back on-line, Kit looked up to see both of her mates standing beside the bed. Damn, they were so fucking hot, loose jersey pants riding low over taunt lower abs had replaced their jeans, the soft fabric exposing matching happy trails that she knew for a fact lead straight to heaven. But as her eyes made their way north muscular arms crossed over broad chests led to stern expressions let her know they'd been *listening in* and were not exactly pleased with what they'd been hearing. *Fuck me, they really don't understand how my mind processes information. Just because I miss something doesn't mean I'd like to go back there...well, at least not most of the time.* Right now, returning to her simpler life sounded like a very good idea.

🐾 🐾 🐾

TREV COULD FEEL Jameson's frustration pulsing all around them—the fact it was overriding his own meant his brother was nearing his breaking point. The negative emotion wasn't going to help their situation and the truth was Trev wasn't sure he could mask his own frustration and keep his brother calm. And unless they kept their heads on straight, they wouldn't be able to discuss this rationally with their reluctant mate.

This had been an ongoing struggle with Kit and he wasn't quite sure how to end the challenge once and for all. *'Let me deal with her. You are too angry and none of us wanted this sort of end to our evening. Remember, she is still coming down from the scene and we don't want to take this too seriously—yet.'*

'Fine, but handle it. I am tired of always worrying that she is going to decide we are more trouble than we're worth.' Trev knew the core of Jameson's anger was his fear of losing Kit, but he also knew she'd never leave them or their children. *'Remember, there is more than one way to leave.'* When Trev didn't respond, Jameson continued. *'She could lock away her heart and I think that might actually be worse. If she regrets being mated, eventually she'll grow bitter and resent us. There are a lot of ways to lose her, brother.'*

Both he and Jameson had wasted far too much time drifting after their parents had been killed. Trev had often thought back on that time and wondered how they'd managed to finally emerge from the fog of grief that had surrounded them. They'd lost months that should have been devoted to building the pack rather than mentally reviewing every move they'd made that night and endlessly sorting through "what ifs". But as much as they wanted to spare Kit from making the same mistakes they'd made, the bottom line was she was an intelligent woman who was more than capable of making her own decisions. *'Well, good fucking luck. I didn't miss that look. When she raises her chin like that there is a battle ahead. I'm going upstairs to the office and vent some of my frustration on the list of slackers I got from the manager at the club.'*

When Jameson turned on his heel and stomped out of the dungeon, Trev tried to hold back his chuckle. Kit's expression softened and he saw some of the starch leave her spine. They could easily block their conversation from her, and she didn't know several of the new-hires at their downtown club were not working out well. What on earth was wrong with people these days? They wanted the income, but didn't want to do any more than the barest minimum? Trev didn't doubt for a minute that the upcoming phone conference with their operations manager was going to leave the man with little doubt about how Jameson felt on the subject.

Trev let several seconds of silence pass before speaking, "Want to explain or would you rather I just started?" He saw Kit wince at his harsh words, but he wasn't going to coddle her this time. She needed to get past this and he was determined to help her even if it meant a departure from the way he usually dealt with her. He hated seeing a cloud of self-doubt pass through her eyes, he didn't want her to doubt herself; he just wanted her to know that her destiny was about her choices, not about circumstances beyond her control.

"I'm sorry. I know my mind wanders and I wish I was better at shielding you from that. I don't want to hurt you..." Trev could hear the sorrow in her voice and nearly folded, but instead he just pulled up a chair and sat down alongside the bed. Folding his arms over his chest he sat back, watching her thoughtfully and simply waited. She'd scooted up so her back was against the carved headboard and he knew it wasn't comfortable, but he planned to leave it alone for the moment. When she started to pull the sheet up to cover herself from his view, Trev simply shook his head. She didn't argue, but since he knew she wasn't cold covering her body from his view was her way of putting distance between them, and that was something he wasn't going to allow.

"I'm just worried..."

When she didn't continue, he inquired, "About?" Her eyes were glassy with unshed tears, and he could feel how unsettled her emotions were. "Talk to me, Kit. I can't help if I don't understand the problem." His words must have struck some cord because he was shocked when she launched herself into his arms. Trev wasn't entirely sure how she had managed to move so effortlessly, hell, it had been impressive even for a shifter.

She didn't cry, but her entire body was shuddering and that was cause enough for concern. Pulling a soft throw from the end of the bed, he wrapped it around her back tucking it all around her and moved silently up the back stairs until he reached their private suite. He'd grabbed the remote control for the fireplace and turned it up before settling on the large leather sofa facing the fire. She curled against him and finally spoke, "I'm scared, Trev. There is so much at stake—so many people's safety and future depend on my ability to be able to separate fact and fiction, and then I have to be able to do whatever needs to be done. I'm not sure I can do any of those things." He didn't respond because he knew her well enough to know she wasn't finished.

Kit processed information at the speed of light, but she didn't work through her emotions nearly as quickly. He'd always suspected she'd learned to distance her mind from her heart as a way to protect herself from the judgment she'd felt as a child, but he would never say that to anyone but Jameson. Everything they'd learned about their mate indicated Kit's mother had been quite harsh, and even though it now appeared as though she'd been trying to protect her daughter, the damage had still been done.

"We all know that I have no idea how I was able to send Damian behind the seal. And if I don't know how I did it there is little chance I'll be able to do it again. And I'm not sure I'm really capable of hurting someone on purpose." She shuddered in his arms and he simply tightened his hold around her shoulders. "It was one thing to react—you know, I didn't even have to think that night. I knew he was going to hurt you and Jameson, and I just acted. But what if I can't really pull that off again if I'm not protecting someone I love?"

"Baby, I think the thing you are forgetting is that the only reason you would need to hurt anyone was to protect those you love. There isn't another reason, is there?" He watched as her eyes widened in surprise, the understanding that moved through her expression was comforting, but he wasn't foolish enough to think those simple words were enough. "I don't think you understand that magic is based on the power of the Universe and that it's been granted to you because your heart will always filter it toward the side of light rather than darkness. It's simply a matter of who you are at your core. You are a good person." He threaded his fingers into her hair at the base of her skull and tightened his grip, tiling her face back so he could look into her eyes. "Your heart knows this, you just need to get your head out of the way. I wish more than anything you could see yourself through the eyes of others—because, oh how different your view would be."

Trev wasn't sure he'd ever meant anything more. And feeling her relax in his embrace, watching as the tension seemed to drain from her facial features, fulfilled a part of him as her mate. Now if he could just help her through the coming weeks when he knew her every move was going to be sliced and diced by far too many people. The scrutiny would probably cause her to question herself, but he hoped they'd made enough progress tonight she'd be stronger the next time she felt vulnerable. "What I want you to remember is that even the strongest person is vulnerable at times. And that vulnerability isn't the same as weakness. Vulnerability keeps you grounded, it means your soul is capable of being open and empathetic, and those are amazing gifts and rock solid strengths."

The single tear that breached her lower lid to slide silently down her cheek reminded Trev of the wax he'd seen his dads use to seal important documents. That tear sealed this moment in a way nothing else could. Slowly lowering his lips to hers, Trev pressed a kiss of promise silently against her warm sweetness. He'd only intended to reassure her that all was well between them, but when she shifted her weight to grind her lush ass against his erection,

Trev felt as if fire had exploded in his blood. He got to his feet without breaking their kiss and didn't release her lips until he'd turned and bent to lay her on the sofa where he'd been sitting. He was far too impatient to walk all the way to their bedroom and he loved watching the various shades of golden light from the fire dance over her ivory skin.

Opening the blanket, he simply stared down at her as he shed his pants. When he lowered himself over her, Kit opened her body to him and he smiled against her lips. "I thank the Universe each and every day for you, baby. We'd looked for you for so long, but you were well worth the wait." He emphasized his last words by thrusting deep into her waiting heat. It didn't matter that shifters lived far longer than humans—an eon wouldn't be enough time with her.

Chapter Seven

Jameson stood in front of the windows of his office staring out into the large open space behind the estate's main house. It had been almost a week since he and Trev had taken Kit to the dungeon and things had gone south so quickly. He was grateful Trev had left their connection open during his conversation with Kit, because it had allowed him to hear for himself what she'd been thinking. Her insecurity had surprised him, and he was grateful he'd let Trev handle the situation. Heaven only knew how badly he would have fucked it up. He'd felt helpless and frustrated and neither of those would have helped.

The fact he absolutely adored his spirited mate didn't mean she didn't drive him to distraction—often. Why she didn't see how perfect they were for her and how much they could help her was a puzzle he didn't seem to be able to fit together. She was much too hard on herself in his opinion, but as Trev had pointed out when the two of them had talked earlier, that wasn't something she was going to overcome overnight. It had taken years for the damage to her self-confidence to take its toll and healing wouldn't come nearly as quickly as he'd like.

He'd sat last night and watched her play with their children, grinning like a fool as the two small magicals practiced their rapidly expanding repertoire of skills. The toddlers were already moving small objects and even though Adana had been the first to show a natural affinity for magic, Ryan was catching up fast. Just a few days ago, Ruby had noted Ryan would be able to match his sister in just a few weeks. Kit had been working with them on shielding themselves from moving objects. She'd explained that her hope was to protect them from one another, but Jameson suspected she was already planning for their future. As he and this brother looked on, they'd wondered if they had ever been that competitive. Ruby's snort of laughter from his side had been all the answer they'd needed.

"You two were the most competitive children I'd ever met. Your mother thanked the Great Goddess above that you weren't magical. I'm not sure either of you would have survived if you'd had magic to use against one another." They'd both laughed because she was right. But even though they'd been fiercely competitive, they'd also been each other's best friend. Jameson didn't know if all twins shared the intense connection they felt, he only knew that his brother was his other half. He remembered talking to his dads late one night after returning from a run. A few of their older friends in the pack were mating and Jameson had been worried about how a third person would change his relationship with his brother.

Both of his dads had listened intently to his concerns and then patiently explained why he needn't worry. That night had been one of the most important lessons they'd ever taught him and he was ashamed he'd forgotten it the other night with Kit. Both of his dads could have easily become frustrated with him for questioning himself and his brother. But they'd calmly listened to his insecurities and validated his concerns while allaying them. *Don't you wish you had followed their example the other night with Kit? You should have opened your heart to the woman who has made you and your brother even stronger as Alphas rather than merely thinking about how her thoughts affected you.*

Taking a deep breath, Jameson turned away from the window and took a mental inventory of their office. He wanted to be sure everything was in place, because today was Kit's first scheduled training session with Devin. Several members of the Supreme Council were due to arrive at any time, and Kit's parents had made an appearance late last night. Jameson and Trev both were finally starting to understand Carla Harris a little better, and while Kit's mother might not ever be one of their favorite people, she seemed to be mellowing as time passed. There was no question that she was a powerful witch, and the fact she'd almost died helping their parents defend them had also played heavily in her favor. But her continual sniping at her daughter was almost more than Jameson could overlook at times.

Moving back behind his desk, he was surprised to see Marcus Hines leaning against the wall by the door. Waving him toward one of the chairs facing his desk, Jameson watched as he sauntered across the wooden floor. The man could move as silently as a soft breeze, something Jameson had always admired, but today it just seemed creepy. His longtime friend and mentor hadn't been back to the estate since the night his role in the drama unfolding around them had been revealed. How Marcus had deceived him for so long was something Jameson had spent a lot of time thinking about—it had been a humbling realization. Why the man hadn't told them about his friendship with Kit's grandfather had been frustrating enough, but the fact he was Damian and Devin's half-brother had nearly been a deal breaker in their friendship.

"To what do I owe this unexpected pleasure?" Jameson didn't even try to keep the sarcasm from his voice. They'd seen Marcus a few times since that night, but things were still decidedly strained between them. Kit had dragged them along when she'd gone to visit after the birth of Marcus and Reagan's son, but they hadn't stayed long enough for any of them to feel comfortable together again.

"You know full well why I am here. I won't let Kit face this alone. I promised her grandfather I'd look after her, and I intend to fulfill that promise—no matter who it annoys." Typical Marcus. He wasn't willing to admit he felt guilty for misleading everyone he'd called a friend. And he had a remarkable way of making this all about him. Fucking narcissist.

Marcus Hines owned one of the most exclusive sex clubs in the country. Memberships were coveted and the fees spoke to the social and economic status of those who could afford them. Marcus had attained a level of success in the lifestyle that most club owners could only dream of, but the fact he was probably several hundred years old probably contributed a lot to his success as well. His expertise was sought after and his financial success was envied, but Jameson had always sensed a restlessness just below the surface—now he knew why.

Stalking back to sit behind his desk, Jameson leaned forward and asked, "Tell me exactly why you are *really* here, Marcus. You don't expect me to just let you waltz out to the meadow and observe, do you? And that is assuming you can get past Ruby, which I personally doubt—she might be little, but she sure seems to have a serious kick ass attitude when it comes to you."

To Jameson's surprise, Marcus actually laughed out loud before responding, "That she does. But to be fair, you need to look at both sides of that story. I'm willing to concede my error in not confiding to you and Trev that I knew where your mate was—even though I still think it played out the way it was intended to. But Ruby is more culpable in this than she is willing to admit. And as for gaining your permission, that's a non-issue because I'm here to protect Kit, not hurt her. All the other factors aside, Kit is still a submissive who is a member of Dark Knights, and that means she falls under my protection when it's within my ability to provide it." Marcus studied his fingernails as if they were suddenly the most interesting thing in the world before looking up and grinning, "Besides, Reagan has been struggling with the whole mommy thing, and I'm hoping to redeem myself a bit in her eyes because as it turns out, I'm not really that much help with the baby."

Jameson couldn't hold back his roar of laughter. Could it be the great and mighty Marcus Hines was being humbled by his own infant son? "You know, that almost makes up for the fucking ass wipe stunt you pulled. Knowing that you have finally found something that you aren't *perfect* at is sweet vindication, for sure. Hell, for years I've worried someone—probably Reagan, was going to nominate you for sainthood."

Marcus chuckled, but before he could respond Ruby stormed into the room. "What do you think you are doing, Marcus? Did the Supreme Council ask you to attend today? Boy oh boy, this chaps my ass I tell you. Why they think you are the best thing since sliced bread I have no idea—it's amazing really that I seem to be the only one who knows what a worm you are. They sent you, didn't they? And has my husband spoken to you from the other side as well?" When Marcus merely nodded, she turned on the heel of her shocking pink high-tops and stomped from the room muttering something about incompetent fools and traitorous ghosts, leaving a trail of smoke in her wake. Kit's strong emotions lit candles, but Ruby seemed to be able to conjure smoke from absolutely nothing. He'd always wanted to ask her about it, but hadn't found a time when he wasn't worried his inquiry might not lead to a visit from the local fire department.

Before he and Marcus could discuss the situation any further, Braden bounced into the room with Cecil Owen trailing close behind. "Hey, I just met Granny Good Witch in the entry and she seemed really pissed." Braden's eyes settled on Marcus and the young wizard stopped so quickly Cecil actually bumped into him. "Well, I guess I know what set her off." Jameson admired the young man's loyalty to his mentor and grinned when Braden's eyes narrowed, "What did you do? You better not have hurt her feelings again."

Cecil settled his long slender fingers over the teen's shoulders and Jameson watched as Braden's muscles seemed to relax right in front of his eyes. The two wizards had become fast friends despite their significant age difference, and watching them interact had Jameson wondering which one was reaping the bigger benefit. Most of the time he considered it a draw. Before he could respond, Trev and Kit entered the room, and they were soon followed by several newcomers, who Jameson assumed were members of the Supreme Council.

Braden had made his way to Jameson's side and snickered, "They are a strange group, aren't they? The first time I met the witches from the Council I wondered if they'd dressed in costumes just to freak me out, but Cecil says they always dress like either *meirdreaches* or flower children—whatever that means." Jameson had to bite the insides of his cheeks to keep his smile to a minimum. He wasn't about to tell the young man *meirdreach* was an Old Irish term for prostitute, so essentially the older wizard had said his fellow Council members dressed like streetwalkers and hippies.

Listening as the Council members rattled on about all the precautions they felt should be in place, Jameson found himself wanting to roll his eyes at the highhanded attitude. How on earth they had so little faith in Kit baffled him. Hell, she was fucking brilliant and her innate goodness wouldn't ever steer her wrong. *Holy fucking hell.* Jameson suddenly felt as if he'd been run over by a truck. He'd been treating her the same way—even though his meddling was coming from a place of love, it really wasn't any different. He owed his sweet mate a big apology—something he intended to provide as soon as possible.

By the time Kit was finally allowed to make her way to the meadow, Jameson knew she was reaching the end of her patience. There were small lines bracketing the corners of her eyes that were always a dead giveaway that she was pushing herself past exhaustion. Pushing his words into her mind was easy since she had very little resistance when tired. *'I'm very proud of you, love. You're going to do great and we'll be nearby if you need us.'* He felt more than heard her acknowledgement and gratitude.

🐾 🐾 🐾

K‍IT WALKED TO the meadow followed by a ridiculous number of *observers* and was almost relieved to see Devin standing at the edge of the ravine. When she got close enough to see his grin, she could only shake her head. "I hope you know this wasn't my doing. Holy horseshoes and hand grenades this is almost as embarrassing as having my mother walk me into for the first day school each year."

Devin leaned his head back and laughed out loud, and Kit was struck by how dramatically it changed his appearance. When he leveled his gaze back on her, he smiled while shaking his head, "Don't worry about it, Kit. I expected this. They don't trust me and I can hardly blame them. But time is on my side and they'll eventually see that I mean you no harm." Kit found herself wanting to believe him, she'd seen the shadows in his eyes that reminded her of a man who had never really felt love and acceptance. In that moment Kit understood how truly lucky she'd been— her upbringing might not have been traditional, but she'd never doubted she was loved. Now she might be frustrated with the dog and pony show behind her, but the simple fact was—each of those people had her back—literally. Her mates' love and acceptance were unquestionable as well. Yes, she'd been blessed beyond measure.

Flashing him a warm smile, Kit leaned forward and whispered conspiratorially, "Well, we'll see, personally I don't think they have much faith in either of us. I'm not sure they trust you to do the right thing, and they don't think I'm smart enough to know when I'm in over my head." When he didn't comment she gave him her annoyed mommy scowl and put her hands on her hips letting know how frustrated she was, then added, "Seriously, they don't think I'll know if you are blowing smoke up my ass, but I will—so don't even try it."

"No, ma'am. Wouldn't even consider it." Kit found herself shaking her head and smiling at his insolence. God, she didn't want to like him, but she could already see herself headed in that direction. *Damn it all to hell.*

Devin spent the next hour briefing Kit on the basics of

the dark side of magic, emphasizing how easily it could be dispelled by light if she'd only use white magic quickly and effectively. Nothing he'd shown her seemed extreme, but there had been short cuts in spell casting that almost seemed like cheating. It was a strange thrill to learn the edgier side of magic and as much as Kit hated to admit it, she was probably enjoying things a little more than she should. For reasons she wasn't sure she wanted examine too closely, she felt a satisfying sense of power using the darker elements of magic.

Before she realized it, dusk was beginning to fall and Kit suddenly felt exhaustion roll over her in a crashing wave. "Don't worry, Kit, we're finished for now. I want you to practice what I've shown you because these steps are the foundation of everything that comes after. These building blocks must be second nature before you can master the more powerful steps that will follow. I know how my brother's magic works and I'm going to give you all the tools you need to defeat him. We'll meet again in two days."

"Why so soon? Has something happened?" The power she'd been feeling moments before had suddenly shifted to fear and Kit felt it stab into her chest, stealing her breath.

"Many things are happening, but Damian is becoming desperate and suspicious. Either of those in and of themselves would be a problem with him, but together they spell disaster. He's barely functional because his anger is far greater than his ability to channel it effectively. Locked alone behind the seal, he has no way to vent the rage that is continuing to boil. He calls his minions to speak with him around the seal, and even though he can't perform the magic himself, he has a rapidly growing group of devoted followers who are happy to do his bidding."

Devin's chin dropped to his chest and Kit could feel him trying to gather his thoughts. The ground beneath her feet rippled and Kit knew Devin was pulling grounding strength from the earth. When he finally raised his face to hers, Kit was surprised to see the pain reflected in his dark eyes. His words were softly spoken but she felt how difficult they'd been for him to utter, "Ask Marcus, perhaps he'll be willing to tell you about our father. He fell into the same abyss of hatred." Once again, Kit noticed sadness and vulnerability in the other wizard's eyes and she wondered what he'd suffered at the hands of his father. She really believed the man standing in front of her was trying to help her, and for that, she was grateful. How isolating it must be to be caught between opposing forces—not being truly accepted by either side.

Kit simply nodded and turned to go, but then thinking again, she turned back, "Devin?" He was already shimmering as he prepared to disappear from the meadow. Kit watched as he settled back into this realm and smiled. "Do you think it would be all right for Braden to tag along next time? He's incredibly gifted and I'd like him to be able to learn with me." She had a feeling any showdown with Damian was going to involved Braden, so it seemed reasonable for him to learn the more practical applications and dangers associated with the dark arts as well. "That is if he's interested and if I can get his guardian's approval—which quite frankly is a pretty big *if*."

She was pleased to see laughter light Devin's eyes when he answered, "Sure, Kit. I understand your reasoning and agree. I'd enjoy getting to know him, he really seems like a great kid—despite his questionable paternal lineage." They both laughed at his thinly veiled reference to the fact Braden was Damian's grandson.

Kit nodded and waved, "See you in a couple of days. Take care." He simply waved and in a swirl of white smoke he disappeared from her view. By the time she turned around to head back to the main house, there were several people standing right behind her. Damn it to destiny she hated it when they snuck up on her like that.

🐾 🐾 🐾

LIBBY WELLS PULLED up in front of the Wolf Pack's enormous mansion and sighed. God she was exhausted, she couldn't ever remember feeling so utterly depleted. Her projects at NYU were nearing completion and she could hardly wait for them to wrap up. She was certainly overdue for some serious R & R, but until she put the final touches on her presentation for the Society of Neuroscience's upcoming conference, Libby really couldn't justify taking any time off. Hell, who was she kidding? She'd been sleeping on the small sofa in her office for weeks because it was usually too late when she was finally finished for the day to justify driving home. Jesus Pete there had been one stretch earlier this month where she hadn't been to her apartment for eight days in a row. Thank God the private bathroom off her office had a small shower.

Opening the door of her small car, Libby stepped out and leaned backward arching her back trying to relieve some of the kinks that came from sleeping on the damned sofa. She gave a loud squeak when strong hands gripped her shoulders and started to massage them. Her startled response was quickly replaced by groans of gratitude as she felt the muscles loosen under skilled fingers. She didn't even need to turn around, Libby knew there was only one man at the estate who would touch her so intimately. She felt his warm breath wash over her ear, "Hi, sweetheart. It's about time you came back to see me. I have someone I want you to meet." His silken voice drifted over her skin and suddenly Libby's body forgot all about the fatigue she'd felt a few seconds ago. Damn her traitorous body for letting her hormones highjack her good sense.

"Well, Charlie, I hate to be the bearer of bad news, but I'm not really here to see you, although I have to admit your fingers are about to weave some powerful magic and I may just ditch the beastie boys and stay right here for the duration of my visit." He chuckled and turned her so she faced him then leaned down to press a heated kiss to her lips. The kiss started as a warm greeting but soon rocketed straight to a smoldering promise of the physical pleasure she well knew he could give her. Frick-fracking fuzzy frogs she needed to get this project wrapped up and sleep for a week on some warm beach while gorgeous cabana boys delivered fruity drinks with those cheesy little umbrellas.

"No can do, sweetness, as much as I'd love to bypass the formalities and fuck you right against the side of your car, that wouldn't come close to sating my hunger for you." Libby shuddered as Charlie kissed a path down the side of her neck before licking over her exposed collarbone. "You meet with our Alphas and then we'll be waiting for you when you've finished." He led her into the chaotic household and Libby couldn't help but wonder if this place was ever really quiet. Charlie leaned forward and pressed his nose to hers and grinned, "Nope, never and that's why Dirk and I live in one of the larger cottages out back."

"That reading people's mind trick is annoying you know. And who is Dirk?" She would really love to study his brain and find out how exactly he was able to hear her thoughts. But of course he'd have to be dead and that seemed like a real waste in her opinion because even if he was too young for her, he was thirty-two shades of hot and flat-out amazing in bed.

She knew he'd heard her when he arched his brow and grinned, "Amazing, huh? And hot? Well, I'm liking how this is working out, but we'll have a chat about that age thing because as you know shifters don't age quickly. I'm probably far older than you think I am. But for now, head on in and talk to Jameson and Trev, they're waiting for you."

By the time she was seated across from Jameson, Libby had been fed a snack that would put most of the meals she'd had the past six months to shame. *One thing you can say about shifters, they eat well...or at least they eat a lot. Must be nice to burn calories like a blast furnace.* Looking up at Jameson, she saw his sly grin and when she glanced to her left she noted a matching one on Trev's face.

"Okay, you two. You got me out here, fed me, and have given me alcohol," she waved her glass of wine at them. "So what's up? You know the deadline I'm trying to meet, so tell me that Kit is okay and I'll be on my way." God she hoped Kit was all right. She felt like the worst friend ever because she really had been so immersed in her project for the past several months she had virtually lost contact with everyone except her grad assistants.

"Kit is fine, she isn't the reason we called you. The project you've been working on is going to gain you some serious acclaim, Libby. You'll be offered a number of lucrative contracts, we just wanted ours to be the first offer you heard." She arched a brow at him wondering what on earth he might have in mind. "First of all, let me congratulate you on your successful project. The implications of your findings are going to put catapult several medical procedures ahead by years. Your findings are going to save a lot of lives."

Libby was well aware Jameson's assessment was point on, what surprised her was the fact he *knew* it. Deciding to wait to see where the conversation was headed, she simply nodded and held her questions hoping he'd hurry up and get to the point. He looked at her and smiled, "We also know there are some implications in your findings for shifters—some rather significant implications that we'd like to see you follow up on. And we're willing to build you a lab and pay you well for your time while you pursue those threads."

She knew her mouth had to have dropped open, but holy shit they had totally blindsided her. Trev chuckled, "Damn, sorta wish we'd videotaped this, I don't think Kit is going to believe us when we tell her that we rendered her best friend speechless." Libby tried to glare at him, but the truth of his words were too much and she couldn't hold back her laugh.

"True that. And I'm going to deny it happened too—it's a matter of pride." Libby paused and took a deep breath as she looked between the two men that looked to much alike it was almost spooky at times. "Damn, I am completely floored. A lab? Really? Do you really have any idea how much that would cost? And I'm not even going to ask how you've gotten access to the results of my research or who has interpreted them so you'd know there are big implications for shifters. A fact I'm not disputing—I'm just surprised you know it, that's all."

Jameson leaned forward, "We've already started building a state of the art medical facility. We're pulling Angie back from the medical center—for a lot of reasons. My brother and I had already been planning to ask her to make the change before her kidnapping, but that showed us just how vulnerable our pack members are when they are away from the estate." Libby watched Jameson's eyes soften as he looked at her intently—studying her closely, and she found herself fighting the urge to fidget under his scrutiny. "She was also working herself to death, much like another brilliant, young woman I know." *Ouch. That hit way too close to home.* He gave her such a pointed look that she found herself swallowing and looking down at her lap. "We need her expertise and she needs to be here. I'm not saying she was entirely thrilled with our plan, but she seems to be warming up to the idea. We'd like the two of you to work together on ways to improve the quality of our healthcare. The number of shifters has seen a rather dramatic decrease in the past decade. We'd like to see that trend reversed."

Jameson slid an envelope over to her, "This is a written offer. Take it with you and open it when you have the time to give it thoughtful consideration." Libby was still struggling to wrap her mind around this turn of events, but she followed their lead and stood when they both got to their feet. Both men extended their hands and she shook them without even realizing what was happening because her mind was spinning with the possibilities. Jameson laughed and tilted his head toward the door, "Charlie and Dirk are pacing outside the door and I don't want to keep you here all evening discussing the details. After you've had a chance to review the offer, give us a call and we'll answer any questions you might have." When she took the envelope, clutching it so tightly the edges crinkled in protest, Jameson smiled and added, "And Libby, I think you'll find that we're pretty eager to make this work." He nodded toward the envelope letting her know the offer was going to be difficult to pass up.

This time it was Trev who spoke up, "And, we're expecting you to have questions so don't hesitate to call with those. And Libby, all things are negotiable—never forget that." Suddenly she wasn't sure they were speaking exclusively about the offer. After all, she knew they were members of Dark Knights and she'd learned enough about the lifestyle to understand all the implications of pre-scene negotiations. Libby wasn't a fool, she knew full well Trev had deliberately left the comment open-ended. She also knew they were going to make the deal so sweet she wasn't going to be able to say no. The only problem was, could she work for two men she knew full well were Dominants? She wasn't a shifter so she wouldn't be subject to their Alpha nonsense, but they'd still be her employers and that would mean she'd have to make some allowances for their bossiness.

She smiled as she made her way to the door, "Well, you've given me a lot to consider," and waving the envelope, she added, "and I'm sure this is going to be quite interesting as well. I'll get back to you as soon as I can. I need to put the final touches on my presentation, and then I'll be flying to San Diego in in a couple of weeks for the conference, but I'll touch base with you before I leave." She shook both men's hands again and shook her head at how lost her hand looked in their grip. "If Kit is available, I'd love to say hi before I leave. And if my godchildren aren't busy terrorizing their nanny, I'd like to see them as well."

Both men laughed out loud, "Kit will be back momentarily, I believe she's been out working with Ruby in the small lab we built for her. The last time she and her granny destroyed the kitchen, we decided it was cheaper to build a separate facility complete with a great fire extinguishing system. It was less costly than our repeated repairs to the kitchen and it keeps the staff from wanting to strangle our mate." Jameson had tried to make light of the situation, but Libby knew Kit had done some significant damage on more than one occasion. She'd also seen pictures of the facility they'd built for Kit to use while learning all her hocus-pocus tricks and the set-up was something to behold. Hell, Kit had been a disaster in the kitchen even without the added risks associated with learning magical spells, Libby didn't even want to think about how much more dangerous she'd been now.

Trev grinned down at her and continued, "As for the *treacherous two*, as most of the pack refers to our children, I'm sure they'd be thrilled to see you. Just don't let them levitate you, they've mastered take-offs but not landings."

Fuck me. Is he serious? Guess I should be grateful for the warning.

Chapter Eight

Kit walked gingerly down the long hallway, trying to make her way quietly past her mate's office when she noticed Charlie and Dirk pacing just outside the door. Sighing to herself, Kit knew that could only mean one thing, her pint-sized pal, Libby, was inside. She'd known Jameson planned to offer Libby a position after her big project ended, but she hadn't realized they'd planned to so this soon. *Damn, nobody ever tells me anything.* When Charlie looked up at her, Kit saw panic move over his face as he froze, "Shit, are you okay? You look sort of...well, worse for wear. What the hell happened? Do our Alphas know you've been injured?"

Damn it, she'd forgotten all about cleaning up before returning to the house. Hell, who was she kidding, she hadn't really been thinking clearly and now that she thought about it, she really didn't even remember making her way back to the house. Looking down at her clothing, she winced at the rips and tears that were highlighted by the black soot. *And what the heck? Who knew buttons would actually melt into the fabric of a shirt?* "Well, there was a small explosion, and," she didn't get to finish her sentence when the ornately carved wooden door behind Charlie slammed open and a very annoyed Jameson stormed out of the office to stand in front of her with Trev right on his heels. *Oh yippee, two pissed off mates for the price of one. Goddess I really don't need this right now.*

"Explosion? Explain." Jameson was in full Alpha-mode and Kit couldn't hold back her involuntary flinch at his harsh tone. Good Goddess she was in for it now. Neither of her mates understood that magic was like anything else—just because you had natural ability, that didn't mean there wasn't a learning curve involved. She'd tried to point out that professional athletes learned and then practiced skills for years before they achieved greatness, but the argument had fallen on deaf ears so she'd given up trying to make the point.

Kit looked from Jameson to Trev and back again before taking a deep breath, "Well, I'm trying to learn how to modulate the amount of dark energy I put out. And well…it seems blenders are apparently particularly sensitive to that sort of thing." She could have sworn she saw the corners of Jameson's lips twitch but it was gone so quickly she wasn't sure. As always a small crowd was quickly gathering around them to see what sort of trouble she'd stirred up this time, and none of them tried to hold back their laughter. *I swear there is some sort of network alert that goes out calling all voyeurs. And if I find a video on YouTube again someone is going to find themselves turned into fucking frog—no there is no imagination in that, I'll have to come up with something out of the ordinary—something truly—*

"Baby? Are you all right?" The concern in Trev's voice was unmistakable and it pulled her back to the moment.

"Yes, I'm fine. Sticky, but fine." *Mostly.* The truth was her ego was probably more damaged than anything else, but she didn't feel particularly obligated to share that little tidbit. And Braden's hysterical laughter when she and her granny had emerged from the lab hadn't helped either. Damn, she was going to talk to Angie about him—that kid had entirely too much free time if he could be hanging around waiting for her to mess up. Sighing to herself, Kit had to admit it wasn't like he'd had to wait long, but she still thought she should be able to blow up a blender without it being front-page news with the whole pack. In her peripheral vision she saw Tristan slip a folded bill to his brother. *Great. Now they were placing bets on me. Just fucking fairy dancing in the dark dandy.*

"Kitten, where is Ruby? Is she alright?" Jameson failed miserably to keep the amusement out of his voice and Kit really wanted to give him a big slap right upside his head.

"She's just dandy." *Because she is far more experienced and dropped a cone of protection over herself at the first hint of trouble. Did she bother to help me? Oh hell no. And the claim that experience is the best teacher was a lame damned excuse if there ever was one.* "She's in the kitchen trying to wrangle another blender from your staff. Seems she'd become a big smoothie fan all of the sudden." *Probably another thing I need to talk to Angie about. If she's going to teach Granny Good Witch all that health food bullshit, she should be the one slurping up that green goop, not me.* "Now, if you'll excuse me, I'd like to go take a shower." *And guzzle a bottle of something with a really high percentage of alcohol before I collapse into bed.*

As Kit started to weave through the growing crowd, she spotted Libby standing between Charlie and Dirk. Each of the man had a hand on one her friend's shoulders holding her back and for the first time she could remember, Kit was actually grateful to be spared one of Libby's rib-crushing hugs. She was still covered in whatever green goo her granny had been mixing up in that damned blender and the scent of burned hair was scorching her sense of smell—damn she hoped she hadn't burned off her eyebrows again. Glancing behind her she frowned, damn it, she'd left green footprints all the way down the hallway.

The cuts she'd gotten from the flying debris were already healing, thanks to the accelerated healing rate of a shifter, but there was still blood on the surface of her skin and spots where it had dripped onto her clothing. She hadn't looked in the mirror, but she knew her red hair was probably sticking out in a hundred different directions leaving her looking like she'd survived a tornado—which wasn't that far from the truth.

She saw Libby start to speak, but Kit just shook her head and mouthed *later*. Libby didn't look pleased, but she finally nodded her assent. As far as Kit was concerned, Libby Wells' biggest gift was her ability to spread joy to those around her but right now Kit just wanted to wallow in the pity party she had planned. Kit had never met anyone who could claim immunity when it came to the little dynamo who was Libby Wells' charm, and when her friend actually got her hands on you, the effect was almost electric. But right now all Kit could think about was making her way upstairs and soaking in a warm bath and drinking a glass or three of wine until her sense of humor returned, because looking at the smirks surrounding her, she couldn't for the life of her see what everyone around her found so damned amusing.

Kit startled at the realization that holding back her temper was taking all her focus and that was something that had never happened to her before. Then she remembered Devin's words of warning, that even dabbling in dark magic could have unintended consequences, including unsettled and volatile emotions. She'd laughed it off at the time, but now she felt trepidation moving through her. The last thing she ever wanted to do was to accidentally hurt anyone who wasn't a threat to the safety of those she loved. But for just a split second her mind had gone to a very dark place when she'd let the wash of anger move over her and that scared her—a lot.

🐾 🐾 🐾

JAMESON LOOKED ON as Kit slowly made her way up the stairs, and put his hand on Trev's shoulder to keep him from following her. "Give her a few minutes to regain some equilibrium. She isn't seriously hurt and right now she is feeling foolish, she just needs a few minutes to herself." Then he turned to address the pack members who had gathered around, "I don't want any of you to mention this to Kit or anyone else for that matter. Let's remember, she'd trying to cram a lifetime's education into just a few weeks' time, and she is doing it in order to protect all of us. I think she deserves our support and our respect." Most of those around him had the decency to look contrite, but several seemed annoyed with the warning and he made a mental note to speak with each of them individually. Perhaps it was time to remind everyone that the pack was only as strong as their weakest member.

🐾 🐾 🐾

TREV MADE HIS way up the stairs as soon as Jameson returned to their office. He couldn't remember ever seeing Kit look as defeated as she had when she'd looked around her as pack members had worked to hold back their amusement at her misfortune. Seeing the sadness as she registered the betrayal reflected in her eyes had made him want to lash out at those who had made her the object of their ridicule. Damn it, she was busting her ass to master the skills she was going to need to protect the very people who were sneering at her. Hell, there were a lot of times her antics had him biting the insides of his cheeks to keep from smiling, but he also tried to make her understand how grateful he was for all her hard work.

There had also been something else in her eyes, a flash of uncertainty laced with fear but she'd shuttered it so quickly he hadn't been able to read it. For all her bravado and apparent self-confidence, she was still a very real woman trying desperately to fit in and earn the respect of her new *family* and that made her more than a little vulnerable to their scorn. He'd felt her pain and disillusionment just before a flash of terror moved though her mind, it wasn't fear of what might happen to her, but a very real fear that she might hurt someone else. Trev wasn't sure what had set her mind on that path, but it wasn't something he intended to let go.

Stepping up to the door of the master bath, he heard her soft sniffles and wanted to pound his fist into the wall in frustration. Their sweet woman already had enough insecurities about being mated, she certainly didn't need their pack adding to that burden. He'd heard Jameson's admonishment to the members who had been looking on downstairs and then his mental inventory of the members whose reactions hadn't set well. Trev could only hope his brother followed through on those come to Jesus meetings he had planned—and sooner rather than later.

Taking a deep breath to calm the internal storm swirling through him and schooling his features, Trev knocked softly before opening the door. Kit was leaning back in the large tub surrounded by bubbles. Her pose might appear relaxed but her entire body was practically quaking with tension. When she saw him, she quickly swiped the soft washcloth she'd been clutching over her face trying to erase the evidence she'd been crying. She might have hidden the tears, but her red-rimmed eyes would have still given her away even if he hadn't heard her soft sobs just a few seconds ago.

He didn't say anything, just quickly set about stripping out of his clothes and then easing into the large tub to settle behind her. Taking the cloth out of her hand, he gently rubbed it over her back and frowned at the bruises he found there. Obviously she'd been battered from all sides and he wondered briefly how much damage the small lab had sustained.

Leaning forward, he pressed his lips softly against her bruised skin, pleased when he felt her relax into his touch. "That's it, baby. Let me love you. Just relax and let me take care of you." He continued his gentle ministrations and then cupped his hands over the shoulders to pull back gently until she was cradled against his chest. Leaning down to press his lips against the damp skin below her ear, he let his words whisper softly against the spot he knew was particularly sensitive, "We are all very proud of you, baby, even when we don't do a very good job of showing you." He hoped she felt his sincerity, and that it would leach from his soul into hers. Trev had felt their heartbeats synchronize as soon as he'd pulled her against his chest, it was a phenomenon their fathers had talked to them about frequently, but they'd honestly assumed their dads were exaggerating—until they'd met Kit.

One of the most challenging things about having a mate as brilliant as Kit was how creative they'd had to be in order to keep her focused on all the progress she was making rather than fixating on all the ways she could improve. They'd tried to show her that bumps in the road were a part of life, they were meant to remind you that perfection wasn't the goal—putting forth your best effort was all anyone should expect. Kit had unreasonably high expectations for herself and a work ethic that often left everyone around her exhausted just trying to keep up with her. Braden had called it correctly when he'd referred to her as a Wärtsilä-Sulzer RTA96. Damn kid had a real affinity for trivia and Trev had been forced to Google it late one night just to find out what the young wizard had been talking about. He'd laughed when he realized his spirited mate had been likened to the most powerful motor ever made. And at 3,209.085 HP, the comparison was probably about right.

Tristan had stepped up behind him and laughed when he'd seen what was on his laptop screen. "I keep telling Nick and Angie we need to limit Braden's internet usage, but I'm not sure it would make any difference. I swear the kid's mind is a fucking steel trap. I've never met anyone who could retain information like he does—it's humbling to say the least. And I shudder to think of what he'll have stored in his head by the time he's thirty." When Trev turned and looked at him with a brow raised in question, their head of security didn't miss a beat, "I know this is one of his favorite ways to say something is kickass strong, what was he referring to that has you Googling when you don't think anyone is around?"

"Kit. He was talking about how hard she works." Trev finally shook his head and smiled. "Damn, can't you teach that kid to speak normally when he is talking to those with IQs closer to average? And I agree with you, I don't even want to consider how much worse he's going to get as he gets older."

"I'm hoping his social intelligence catches up and he learns to be a little more diplomatic, or at least more aware of the fact he isn't spending all his time with a bunch of Mensa think-tank hopefuls." Trev knew Tristan Michaels was incredibly bright, and his brother, Nick, would likely test in the genius range. And everyone knew the men's mate, Angie, was, without question, the most intelligent person in a pack that had more than its fair share of brilliant members.

Trev hadn't even realized he'd left the telepathic link between them open until he heard Kit's whispered words, "There might be a lot of intelligence floating around, but not much kindness, and that just sucks if you ask me." Kit had spoken so softly Trev probably wouldn't have heard her if he had been a shifter blessed with superior hearing. He wrapped his arms around her and just held her for several minutes, after all, what was he going to say? He certainly couldn't argue her point.

"Come on, sweet baby, let's get you out of the tub. The water isn't warm enough anymore, you'll get stiff and sore if we don't keep you warm." He hated the idea of her being sore, but there wasn't much he'd be able to do to prevent it. "How are your sessions with Devin progressing?" He felt her stiffen under his hands and knew their harsh words when she'd had first agreed to work with the wizard were still a sticking point between them. Trev hated the fact he hadn't been able to breach the chasm they'd created, but it would take time for her to feel comfortable enough to discuss it freely with either him or his brother.

Using his fingers to grip her chin, he turned her face toward his own and framed her heart shaped face with the palms of his hands letting his fingers spear into the soft tresses of her auburn hair. He had to wait several heartbeats for her eyes to raise and meet his, another thing he hated more than he could say. "Listen to me and listen closely, baby. I'll likely go to my grave as an old man regretting the way my brother and I reacted when you told us about the bargain you'd made with Devin. Fear does that to men who love their mate with everything they have—it makes them unreasonable and nastiness spews out of their mouths before their brains are fully engaged in the process." Unshed tears made her eyes glisten, but she didn't respond.

"We hurt you and that is something we'd both sworn to you we'd never do. I'd like to amend that promise right now. We'll never intentionally hurt you—but, baby, we *will* make mistakes. We're not perfect and we'll probably fuck up again—in fact, it's likely. But I can promise you, we'll *always* have your best interests at heart. Our love and respect for you will never be in question, just our ability to express it appropriately. Remember, we're wolves at heart, so civility isn't always the first thing that comes out." Who was he kidding? Civility evaporated the minute anything threatened Kit or their children, it simply ceased to exist. All their parents' training, all those lectures on leadership and how to treat others, most importantly their mate— were suddenly wasted effort on their parts. He could almost feel his mother smacking him upside the head every time he thought back on how they had reacted when Kit announced she'd be working with Devin. *Yeah, not exactly a stellar moment in your relationship, was it?*

"I understand. I really do. But you have to remember, trust is a two way street. You expect me to trust you with my life, but you aren't willing to trust me to protect you in return. You both conveniently forget that I functioned on my own for many years without your protection...actually it's only been since I met you that I actually *needed* protection of any sort." Trev felt his hackles come up, but if he was honest with himself he'd have to concede that even though he didn't like her last statement one bit, it was in fact true.

Before Trev had time to respond he heard the soft scrape of a boot over the polished wood plank floor. Looking over Kit's shoulder he saw Jameson leaning against the doorframe. His posture was deceptively casual, but the pose didn't fool Trev. Looking back at Kit, she rolled her eyes, "He's standing right behind me, isn't he?" When Trev nodded, she let out a long sigh making her sound more like a condemned prisoner headed to the gallows than a mate who was about to be fucked into oblivion. Jameson nodded subtly letting Trev know he agreed, they both knew they had some ground to make up with their lovely wife.

Chapter Nine

Damian had been pacing for hours waiting to hear from the young witch he'd planted inside the Wolf estate. When she'd come to him several weeks ago asking how she could help, he'd first suspected the woman had been sent by the Supreme Council, but the longer he'd talked with her the less convinced he'd been that she was a spy. As near as Damian could determine, Talia was ridiculously ambitious, and he known right away precisely how to exploit that trait at every turn. He wasn't foolish enough to think she was loyal to him personally—no, she was loyal to her ambitions and nothing else. Damian would never *trust her*, but he'd sure use her. Yes, indeed, he knew exactly how to deal with a personality that so closely mirrored his own.

When he finally felt the presence of another person on the other side, he stopped and waited. "Master Damian? Are you there?" Damian was anxious to see the woman who had been feeding him information—to see if she was as soft as her voice. If she looked anything like she sounded, he just might find other uses for her as well. He certainly wasn't opposed to indulging in the pleasures of women, he just didn't see any reason to keep them around after they'd served their purpose.

Damian had always known it was best to speak with people face to face because it was so much easier to determine how honest they were. And at the very least he could know whether or not the other person was intimidated enough to do his bidding. But Kathleen had made that impossible and at this point, he had very few options. The only person he'd ever come close to trusting was Devin, but even his brother's loyalty was seriously questionable.

"Yes, Talia, I have been waiting for you. Do you have any information for me?" Damian knew he sounded rude, but he wasn't at all interested in being her friend so he wasn't going to bother with social niceties beyond the barest minimum. He wanted to know what she'd learned so he could decide how to proceed. There weren't many options, but there were a few and the simple truth was he was going completely insane being trapped behind the seal Kit locked him behind. Damian didn't give a shit that she didn't seem to know how she'd done it—she had two very simple choices, she could join him or die.

"I do and I'm afraid it isn't good. Your brother has been meeting with Mrs. Wolf. Even though I haven't been able to gain access to the part of the estate where they are meeting, the rumors among the staff consistently center on the meetings being some sort of training sessions." *What the fuck? My brother is training her? In what? And why wouldn't he tell me he was spending time with her?* The rage that filled him was so all consuming the stone lined walls surrounding him vibrated and shifted precariously. This time when the witch spoke, her voice was filled with uncertainty, "Are you all right? Do you want me to continue looking into this or…" she let her words trail off and Damian tried to get his anger under control. He didn't want to alienate her, hell she'd actually displayed an incredible amount of courage in her willingness to be the bearer of bad news. Most of his followers wouldn't have dared broach the subject of his brother's possible defection. Damian might not pose a direct threat at this point, but he could still order her execution, so she'd taken a risk in telling him news she would have known he wouldn't like. He might need others to carry out his orders, but Goddess knew he didn't intend to be stuck behind the damned seal forever.

He took several deep breaths to calm himself before answering her, "Yes, I'm fine, just disappointed that he hasn't mentioned the fact he's working with her." It was an enormous understatement and something he intended to address with his *dear brother* immediately. There was still the possibility that Devin was training her to join them, but that seemed like a remote chance since he hadn't told Damian what he'd been doing.

"Please continue your surveillance. Report back to me anytime you see or hear anything—and I do mean anything. Something that might seem insignificant to you might be the final piece of a puzzle for me." Damian took another calming breath before adding, "And Talia, I'm sure I don't have to remind you that your discretion is of the upmost importance." He took a steadying breath before softening his tone, "And I can't tell you how much I appreciate your help. You'll be well rewarded—you have my personal pledge." *Hell, depending on how she looks, she might get far more than my personal pledge.*

🐾 🐾 🐾

DEVIN STOOD IN the dark shadows deep in the cave and listened as the young witch he'd seen lurking around the Wolf's home spoke with his brother. He didn't know what her position was at the estate, but the fact she'd been able to fool everyone was a clear indication that she was a worthy foe. She'd just hung him out with her words and he fully intended to make sure she paid dearly for it. What he hadn't decided was whether to take her out himself, turn her over to the Wolf brothers, or perhaps offer her up to the Supreme Council. Since all three options were likely to end up with the same result he leaned toward simply taking care of it himself—but he had to admit, shifting the karma burden off his shoulders also held a lot of appeal. Hell, he would already spend the next several lifetimes trying to make up for the mistakes he'd made. Devin had spent his entire life lost in the shadows of his brothers. First his father had tirelessly compared him to Marcus—the genius son who had been blessed with all his father's talent, but who'd been "brainwashed" by his mother to walk in the light rather than owning the night. After Marcus had been deemed beyond saving, dear old dad had focused on Damian.

Damian had quickly replaced Marcus and become their father's golden child. Devin's older brother mastered the dark magic so quickly he'd soon been a stronger wizard than his own father, but before that could turn the two into competitors, their father had become ill. When Damian had gone to Europe to study with mentors, he'd caused havoc in every location where he'd been stayed. Rather than being angry as Devin had expected, their father had been enormously proud of his son's "exploits and conquests". Even now, knowing his father's mind had been awash in the pain medication it still rankled Devin that he'd been encouraged to follow Damian's example.

Knowing his brother as well as he did, Devin knew waiting for Damian to cool down wouldn't work—hell, it would actually have the opposite effect. Damian had inherited their father's temper and giving him any additional time to "stew" was just asking for the trouble to mushroom into something resembling a nuclear holocaust. After the mousy young witch quickly scurried away like the rodent she was, Devin stepped up to the seal.

"Damian, I've come to speak with you." Best to take control of the situation quickly. Devin felt the granite floor beneath his feet shift slightly and knew his brother was barely containing his rage.

"Where have you been? I've been waiting on a report since you lost the good doctor." *Oh, so that's how he's planning to play this, huh?*

"I've been spending time with Kit and Braden." Devin knew the mention of his grandson would give Damian pause. His brother had chased the young boy all over the globe trying to secure him. But at some point it appeared Damian's focus had shifted to eliminating the young wizard, and Devin wasn't entirely certain what had transpired to cause his change of heart. "I've been allowed to come and go at the Wolf estate. At first, I was watched continually and all of our training sessions together were closely monitored. But as time has gone on, I've been allowed more time with the two of them alone." Devin didn't intend to tell his brother that the trust he was earning was well founded. He had no intention of helping his brother kill thousands of innocent people just to gain power he didn't deserve. Thinking about Damian gaining control of the Supreme Council and ruling the magical world was the stuff of Devin's worst nightmares.

"Training? Explain," Damian's voice was still laced with anger, but the ground was no longer vibrating.

Devin spent the next several minutes blowing massive amounts of smoke up his brother's ass in reference to his training sessions with the two magicals they needed to further Damian's cause. He wouldn't tell Damian what he was actually doing, but the longer he could stall, the safer everyone would be.

"They have agreed to assist me? Both of them?" Damian's voice was filled with doubt, even as his questions belied his hope. It was moments like these that Devin wished his brother could still be saved from himself. The moments of lucid behavior, brief glimpses of the brother Devin had once admired, always sent pangs of longing through his heart. No matter how justified, it was always difficult to watch those you love pay for their misdeeds and Devin wasn't looking forward to helping bring about his brother's downfall.

By the time he left the cave, he was sure of two things: first, his brother wasn't yet convinced there wasn't more to the story, and second, he needed to speak with someone at the Wolf estate immediately about the young woman he'd seen earlier.

🐾 🐾 🐾

JAMESON WOLF HATED the undeniable knowledge that he'd let Kit down. She was smart, beautiful, kind, and more than capable of taking care of herself—most of the time. But none of that mattered now. Now he and his brother needed to find a way to rebuild the trust they'd damaged, and he knew that wasn't going to be easy.

He and Trev had searched for years for their mate, and when she'd finally walked into their lives they'd vowed to do everything in their power to protect her. And then the first time she throws them a major curveball, not only do they strike out, but they strike out at her.

Jameson had always envisioned an obedient mate who would bear their children, be adored by the members of their pack, and be perfectly submissive. He should probably count his lucky stars they'd gotten two out of three. Trev's laughter resonated in his mind and Jameson had to work to hold back his smile. *'You know she'd kick your ass if she heard that, right? I can already hear the word Neanderthal bouncing around.'* Sighing to himself, Jameson knew Trev was right, but it didn't change the fact it was true. And right now there were sparks already starting to dance in her eyes.

Kit still became frustrated with their telepathic communication from time to time. Even though they often included her, most of the time it was so natural to just let things to flow between them, they often forgot to open the link—and this time that oversight had probably saved his ass. Trev kissed Kit quickly and then turned her to face Jameson. "Kitten? Want to tell me what happened?" He held out his hand as he'd asked the question and was pleased when she placed her much smaller one in his. Closing his fingers over hers, he pulled her closer and brushed the soft auburn tresses back behind her ear. God, he loved her hair, there were so many shades blended together giving it a depth that seemed to shift with even the smallest movement. It felt like the finest silk between his fingers as he threaded his hand through the strands to tilt her face up to his. He loved how her hair flowed to the middle of her back in gentle waves and in the mirror behind her, he could see it reflecting even the smallest amount of light. Kit was gorgeous, there was no doubt about it, but the best part was her beauty seemed to bubble to the surface from deep within and that was beauty that would never fade.

Her small shoulders fell and she slowly shook her head.

"Come on, kitten, I want to know what happened. I'm not judging, and as long as you aren't hurt everything else can be repaired or replaced." She'd dropped her eyes to the floor and he was surprised to see tears in her eyes when he tilted her face back up to his.

"It's not that it is really that bad per se. It's just that it's so damned embarrassing. Sometimes I really want to kick my mother's skinny ass for not starting my training years ago. The learning curve sure would have been a lot easier now if she had." Jameson agreed with her, but there wasn't anything to be gained by rehashing that now. "There are so many basic skills I haven't mastered yet and here I am trying to add dark magic to the mix—and as it turns out the control required for that is even more difficult than white magic." He watched as she appeared to turn her frustration inward. "I should have just started working with one of my mom's friends when I was old enough. But since I obviously had my head up my ass and didn't do that, I guess I'm just as much to blame as she is. Damn, this whole thing sucks big brass balls, I tell you." Jameson knew he'd never unravel all the remarkable aspects of Kit's personality. Hell, just keeping up with her was challenging enough—her mind worked at the speed of light and wasn't anywhere close to being that linear.

"And you know what really worries me? Well of course you don't because I haven't told you yet. Goddess, I really shouldn't have taken that aspirin." Jameson didn't bother to hold back his smile. Kit was the only person he'd ever met who was so sensitive to the little white pills that she'd actually sleep for hours after taking just one. Looking over at Trev, he nodded when his brother tapped his left wrist. Even though he wasn't wearing a watch, the message about time being of the essence was clear. Yeah, if they didn't get her between them quickly, they'd miss the opportunity to make love to her—the thought had his cock twitching in protest.

"That's enough introspection for tonight, kitten. I want to push all of those concerns right out of your head so you'll sleep peacefully and the best way to do that is for us to remind you how much you are loved." Jameson nodded to Trev and chuckled at her squeak of surprise when she suddenly found herself swept up into his brother's arms. While Trev got their mate settled, he quickly stripped out of his clothes, and was in and out of the shower in record time.

Stepping back into the bedroom, he was happy to see Kit teetering on the verge of an orgasm as Trev's rolled tongue disappeared into her vagina in rapid thrusts that were a prelude to coming attractions. Jameson leaned over giving her the command to come just before sealing his lips over hers, capturing her scream and swallowing it down. He and Trev thrived on her pleasure, they'd become addicted to it after they'd taken her the very first time. Everything about her release fed their own arousal—the way she panted, the way she screamed their names, the smell of her sex as it creamed for them. But the sweetest part was the way she trusted them so completely during those moments when she let reality slide away and lost herself in the physical pleasure. Kit's body knew she was safe in their care, even when her mind tried to overrule it, her body followed its instinct and surrendered beautifully.

Kissing a line from the corner of her mouth to her ear, Jameson whispered, "You come so beautifully. I love the way your body flushes and the scent of your honey surrounds us, driving me insane with need. But most of all, I love the way you let yourself go—the trust you give us is an enormous gift, a gift we treasure and intend to cherish always." They hadn't seen much progress in the trust department recently, but Jameson had no intention of giving up. He tried to remember that baby steps were better than losing her—because that simply wasn't an option.

Chapter Ten

Kit's body felt like it was on fire. Trev had threatened to tie her to the damned bed if she didn't hold still before the blasted man had set about shattering her control. Hell, he might as well be using some kind of plastic explosive because there wasn't a chance in hell she'd have enough self-control to last until they were both satisfied—damn insatiable men. Drown them, she worked out almost every day and their endurance was still far superior to hers. They'd gloated about because they were the mighty Alphas...blah, blah, blah. Personally she was still convinced her original assessment of them as sex maniacs was perfectly accurate. Trev pulled back just enough from the throbbing lips of her to grin, "Insatiable sex maniacs? Only for you, baby. We want you to know how much we love you, and this just happens to be one of our favorite ways to show you."

If her mind hadn't been so fragmented by the pleasure he was bringing her, Kit might have snorted indignantly at his attempt to justify their sex drive. Hell, everybody knew shifters were extremely sexual creatures, but even taking that into account, her mates were overachievers. Just as Trev curled his tongue and plunged it deep into her vagina, Jameson stepped up to the bed. Brilliantly colored sparkles of light exploded behind her eyelids and somewhere in the back of her mind Kit realized her senses were starting to overload, the feelings bombarding her were too much for her mind to process, so when Jameson gave her the command to come, the last threads of her control snapped and broke free. In the back of her consciousness she heard a muffled scream but it was several seconds before the fog of lust surrounding her lifted enough for her know the scream had been her own.

Thank the Goddess above Jameson had swallowed the sound in a scorching kiss since her parents were staying in the guest suite directly above them. She'd learned a very embarrassing lesson about discretion the first time her parents had visited. Her mother had used the pack's morning meal as her own personal stage, launching into an animated monologue about how the noises coming from below their bedroom had kept her awake most of the night. Kit's father had tried to change the subject, but Carla hadn't let it go until Kit had finally run from the room with tears of mortification streaming down her cheeks. Jameson had been livid with her mother, and according to several witnesses, her Alpha mate had railed at his new mother-in-law for her disrespectful treatment of her daughter. Trev had followed her upstairs, then tried to cheer her up by beating his chest and assuring her their pack mates would consider her noisy response a point of honor for her mates. He'd strutted around their suite with his chest puffed out like a peacock expounding on the sexual expertise of shifters and how anything less than a Richter registering orgasm would be a legitimate cause for embarrassment.

Kit hadn't wanted to laugh at his antics—Goddess knew he didn't need any encouragement, but she hadn't been able to hold back the giggles that felt like a relief valve. It was the first time she'd truly understood the advantages of having two mates—well, an advantage that wasn't directly linked to her libido. There had been something both empowering and calming in the knowledge that one mate was downstairs acting as her knight in shining armor, while the other was playing the role of court jester.

A sharp nip to the inside of her thigh brought her quickly back to the moment. When Kit opened her eyes, her gaze locked on Jameson's intense dark eyes. His expression wasn't angry as she'd feared it might be since her mind had wandered once again, instead his eyes reflected love and contentment. "Kitten, I can't tell you how much that story meant to us. Knowing we've made a positive difference in your life fills our hearts with joy." Kit was stunned. How could they not know how much she loved them? How could they doubt that her entire world revolved around her mates and children? Sure, she loved her parents and Granny Good Witch, but that paled in comparison to her feelings for Jameson, Trev, and their twins. *Perhaps you spend so much time focused on yourself...what you want to do and the insignificant things you lost in the bargain, that you've forgotten how important it is to be grateful for what you have?* The realization of how selfish she'd been was a bitter pill to swallow, but she vowed to make certain that in the future they knew how much she appreciated everything they did for her.

🐾 🐾 🐾

JAMESON HAD HELD his hands still against Kit and listened to her mind spinning at a pace that nearly made him dizzy. She was so genuine, that her mind was almost an open book and, if he was actually touching her, it was almost as if she were speaking aloud. She'd gone from a screaming orgasm to run a full gambit of emotions in less than two minutes. He appreciated the fact she was incredibly intelligent and it really was a marvel to listen to her process information and work through a problem or her feelings. What he hadn't liked was the fact she now felt guilty for their insecurities—that certainly hadn't been what he'd intended and he was sure that wasn't the direction Trev had wanted this to go either.

One of the things that troubled him about her foray into the dark arts was the fact her emotions now seemed to vacillate from one extreme to the other at the slightest provocation. Kit had never exhibited that lack of control before—hell, she hadn't even been this unpredictable while she'd been pregnant with Ryan and Adana. *'I agree with you, brother. She has been fighting some kind of internal battle ever since she began training with Devin, but Ruby mentioned this was one of the reasons the Supreme Council was so concerned. Apparently the dark arts are a temptation that few can fully combat, and when that resistance is shredded, so is the person's emotionally stability.'*

Jameson wasn't surprised Trev had already noted the change and spoken to Ruby about it, he'd always been far more attuned to the emotional side of those around them than Jameson had. *'I understand the importance of what she is trying to do, but I'm more worried about her now than I was when I thought the threat was simply physical.'* Worrying about her emotional health was something far more frightening, because he had no idea how to help her recover from that type of damage.

Kit wiggled beneath their hands and Jameson realized she had come back from her own wandering thoughts to find they'd taken a little detour themselves. He could see the gray clouds of unease in her eyes and was pleased to see them clear somewhat when he smiled at her. "I don't feel like I've been very honest with you and Trev." Kit's words were spoken quietly but he hadn't missed the hesitance and vulnerability he heard in them. He didn't respond, just watched her thoughtfully as she bit her lower lip. That nervous habit sent a surge of blood into his already aching cock and Jameson worried his brain wasn't going to be fully functional with a diminished blood supply. Fuck, the woman could turn him on just by breathing.

"I feel like an ungrateful shrew. You are both so wonderful to me, and I seem to give you no end of trouble." She took a deep breath and Jameson fought the urge to comfort her when he saw the sheen of tears in her pretty green eyes. But, he knew she wasn't finished and both he and his brother owed her the chance to speak her piece. They were usually busy telling her what they thought was best, perhaps the better plan would be to simply listen and offer guidance only when she asked for it. Jameson made an effort to move closer so his body was wrapped around her protectively and he softened his expression, but still didn't speak.

"I really am grateful for all you do, and for your patience. I know it doesn't seem that way when you hear my thoughts wishing for a simpler life. When I make that wish and relate it back to before we were mated, it doesn't mean I think being mated is what caused the problems. I just wish our lives together, and mine as a witch, wasn't complicated by all this nonsense. It's exhausting and I feel like I'm working all the time and not making any real progress. But worst of all I'm not giving the four people I love the most in the entire world enough of my time and attention. And that is simply unforgivable."

When he opened his mouth to speak, she placed her hand gently against his lips, "No. Wait, please." She shifted her gaze to Trev and spoke again, but Jameson could feel the effects of the aspirin beginning to take its toll. "I always swore I'd never be like my mother, always gone off doing something important for the magical community, but never available for her own family. And then what do I do? Exactly the same thing. It's humbling to see how easy I followed in the footsteps of the person who I least wanted to emulate."

Wrapping his fingers around her dainty wrist, Jameson moved her fingers enough to push them into his mouth and nip softly at the tip of each finger. When he pulled them back he smiled, "Kitten, I'm glad you are happier than you have seemed these past few months, but I'm not pleased that you are putting yourself under so much pressure. You are running the risk of burning yourself out. We stood back far too long when Angie was doing the same thing, but we won't make that same mistake with you."

Trev had moved up along Kit's other side and used his fingers to turn her chin his direction, "Baby, we know your work is important, hell, it would be nearly impossible to gauge the long term significance of what you are undertaking. But the bottom line is, you have to take care of yourself before you can take care of anyone else." When Kit didn't respond, Trev grinned. "Think of it this way, if you were trying to save someone who was drowning and they started pulling you under with them, you would have to back away and get yourself in a safe position before you could help them. This is much the same, you can't help everyone else if you are running on empty."

Kit smiled even as her eyes filled with tears. Jameson

rolled to his back and pulled her against his chest. "Now, before you fall into a dead sleep, I need to feel you wrapped around me, love. I want to be buried so deep inside you that I feel each beat of your heart. Trev and I are going to love you until I have to catch your screams as our names burst past these sweet lips." She settled over his raging hard-on and he slipped into the tight channel slowly. She was soaking wet, but he wanted to savor each pulse and quiver of the muscles lining her vagina as he eased inside.

Jameson had been a Dom almost from the very beginning of his sexual life, and he'd fucked more women during the years since than he wanted to remember. He'd been known as a formidable Dom, his ability to pound into a woman without chasing his own orgasm had become a point of pride during those years. But everything was different with Kit. Jameson still loved their time in the dungeon and playing with her was the hottest sex he'd ever had, but making sweet love to her—the connection he felt between them when things were slow and sensual was earthshattering each and every time. He'd never experienced the joy of soul baring intimacy until he'd made love to Kit. He and Trev had both marveled at the difference one night after she'd fallen to sleep. They'd sat on the small balcony terrace off their bedroom watching the moon move across the sky, and wondered how they'd ever lived without her.

Kit's body was already drawing him in deeper and when he felt the tip of his bulging crown press against her cervix, Jameson felt his chest vibrate with a growl as his wolf began pushing to surface. The full moon was nearly upon them and he was already feeling the need to run with Kit. He and Trev hadn't been able to take her in the meadow for several months and their wolves were feeling the loss. He'd be sure they didn't miss the next opportunity.

Pulling her forward, Jameson used his nose to burrow under her soft hair to speak close to her ear. He felt her shudder in his arms when the warmth of his breath brushed the sensitive shell of her dainty ear, "Kitten, your body is tugging me in so deep, I feel as though you are taking me clear to your soul." Her vaginal muscles clamped down on him like a vise and he felt his eyes roll up until he wondered if he wouldn't lose sight altogether. "Fuck me, you are killing me, love. Death by sensual overload. Damn, what a way to go." Then speaking to Trev, he nearly snarled, "Trev, you need to sink into our mate before she sends me over the edge and you don't even get to play. But I'm warning you, her body is needy and she's going to rock our worlds in short order."

Chapter Eleven

Nobody had to tell Trev twice to sink his cock into his mate, hell no, he was more than ready for this moment. He'd already placed the lube within reach and the minute he moved into position, Kit arched her back giving him a view of her dark pink rear hole that caused the breath to rush from his lungs. "God Almighty, you have the most perfect ass in the entire world, baby. I know you don't believe me, but your pretty pink hole is absolutely stunning. You've pushed back perfectly, opening yourself up to me and I'm humbled at how you take us both into your body and lead us straight to heaven's gate."

All the time he'd been speaking he'd been rubbing lube into the tight ring of muscles surrounding her rear hole. He could only hope his tender touch and preparation conveyed his desire to take his time and love her, because he knew the minute he shoved himself into her heat all bets were going to be off. There was no better feeling than knowing Kit was fully submitting herself to them. Seeing her arch her back to welcome his cock made the wolf in him want to howl in triumph. He'd heard Jameson's silent vow to run under the coming full moon and Trev couldn't wait to fuck their mate in the meadow, and bask in the light of the moon as they had the night they'd officially become mated. And even though it might not make any sense, he wanted to feel his razor sharp canines sink into the tender flesh where her shoulder and neck met. He knew he'd never tire of seeing his and his brother's marks of possession on Kit's creamy skin.

"Oh, Goddess of Light, please. Please, Trev. Move. I'm dying to feel you inside me. I'm afraid I'm going to stop breathing if you don't push in until I can feel your balls pressing against me. I'll feel like I'm being split in two, but it's the sweetest torture in the entire world." Kit's voice was lust-filled and raspy from the panting breaths she was taking, her skin was flushing perfectly, and Trev could feel her already pushing back her release.

"Don't you dare come, baby. Not yet. Hold it back for us. Wait for it, it'll be so much better, I promise you." He knew Kit's mind was already so awash in endorphins she was fighting a losing battle to stave off the orgasm that was threatening to overwhelm her much longer. But the longer she could wait the more intense it would be, and they all three needed the strength of this moment to meld them back into one. As soon as he'd sunk in all the way, he felt his brother begin to move. The feeling of his cock sliding along the other side of the thin membrane separating them set off sparks of fire that moved from Trev's cock straight into his balls causing them to pull up painfully.

Goddamn, at this rate he was going to be the first one to come and he'd only just gotten to the party. What was it about fucking Kit that pushed his control right out the window? Hell, he and Jameson had given subs so many screaming orgasms they'd passed out before either one of them had let go. But their sweet mate ignited a fire in his gut that always turned into a raging inferno within seconds. "Fuck me, I haven't felt this close to being a one-stroke wonder since I was a teenager. Goddamn, baby, you blow my control to hell—I should paddle you for that alone. Your ass clenches me so tight when I pull back, as if it's trying to keep me buried deep inside. But then it flares open like a bloom opening under the warm summer sun, just waiting to welcome the heat it knows is heading its way."

🐾 🐾 🐾

KIT TRIED TO concentrate on Trev's words hoping they would distract her from the fire she could already feel surging through her blood, but damn it, the man wasn't about to make her come just from his words alone. Where was her teasing mate when she needed him? Drown them both for being so perfect. "Oh fuck, kitten, now you've done it—his ego already knows no bounds. Of course your assessment of me is spot on." Jameson's words were clipped but there was still a trace of humor lacing through them. She shouldn't have been surprised at their sudden reversal of roles, it never ceased to amaze her how quickly they could assume the other's personality as if it were their own. But her reflection on the implications of her mates' twin characteristics was cut short by her body's response to their efforts to send her over the moon with a release that was probably going to melt her bones.

Trev was beginning to lose his tightly held control as his pace began to accelerate. With each stroke back into her anal passage, Kit felt herself slide a little further into that fogged state of bliss where nothing but pleasure existed. Kit had heard the submissives at Dark Knights refer to it as sub-space, but personally, she thought the term was entirely inadequate. Hell, even knowing "sub" referred to submissive, Kit still couldn't bring herself to think of reaching nirvana as "sub" anything. Oh no, this wasn't anything close to "below", this was more akin to being launched into the stratosphere where the brightest supernovas zipped by as if they were racing to a newly assigned position in the heavens. This was a place where pleasure and pain were so closely aligned they may as well have been merged together. Kit heard a ferocious growl and was startled back from the edge by the realization it had come from her own throat. Looking down at her fingers, she realized they look more like the claws of her wolf than her hands, the red dots of blood on Jameson's chest attested to the fact she'd sunk them into his chest without even realizing it.

"Oh, my sweet mate, don't ever worry about marking either of us. We'll wear those marks with pride because we'll remember exactly how we earned them." Jameson's voice was raspy and Kit knew he was struggling to hold back his own release. Trev's breathing was labored behind her and she could only pray that he was close because there wasn't any way she hold back the orgasm that was already causing her womb to spasm. When the surface of her skin began to tingle, Kit felt Jameson's hands bracket the sides of her head and pull her down, sealing his lips over hers.

There hadn't been more than a heartbeat between the press of his warm lips over hers and the primal scream she felt burst from her chest. Kit had experienced intense orgasms countless times with her mates, but this was something far beyond anything she'd ever known before. This was a fusion of their souls, an almost ethereal melding of their beings and Kit felt the emotional firestorm that burned their names into her heart as if they'd actually been branded there. Both men followed her over the edge and in the back of her mind their muffled shouts of release brought her an even greater sense of satisfaction. The intensity of the moment slid quickly into oblivion and Kit felt her eyes flutter open to meet Jameson's dark orbs, they were filled with love, but her mind had barely had time to register the concern that filled them when the darkness at the edges of her vision closed quickly to the center and she fell into the respite of sleep.

🐾 🐾 🐾

JAMESON WASN'T SURPRISED when Kit's eyelids slowly lowered and he felt her mind drift into a deep sleep. The last several weeks had been difficult for her and then everything that had happened earlier in the day had been a tipping point. Added to the incredible sex they'd just shared—hell, it was a wonder the whole lot of them weren't in a coma. They took turns cleaning up, because he nor Trev ever wanted to leave Kit alone in the bed after they'd made love to her. She was incredibly strong, but the crash she always had after being taken by them together invariably left her feeling particularly vulnerable. From their first night together they'd vowed to make sure one of them always held her after they'd taken her at the same time. Jameson loved the way she burrowed closer, as if she couldn't get enough of his touch, feeling her settle when he tightened her in his embrace was one of the most satisfying things he had ever experienced, and it certainly wasn't one he'd willing give up. When he returned to the bed he couldn't help looking down on the two people he loved above all others, save his children, and for just a moment he was overwhelmed. He'd dreamed of this for so long there were still times when he just could barely grasp the fact he'd been blessed with so much after feeling as though he'd never smile or laugh again. After they'd lost their parents, Jameson and Trev had both struggled to regain their footing—hell, it had taken months and months for them to bounce back to anything that even vaguely resembled their normal selves.

There had been too many people to remember who had tried to engage them, friends who had worked tirelessly to draw them back into the fold, and attempted to remind them of all they had. But it had been Marcus Hines who had really helped them see how self-destructive their grief had become. Their friend and mentor had been brutally honest, telling them to step back, get their shit together, and get on with the life their parents would have envisioned for them. Little had they known at the time, Marcus had actually known exactly what their parents had wanted for them because they'd been personal friends.

As he started to climb into bed he noticed the message light blinking on his phone and, against his better judgment, he picked it up and then instantly wished he hadn't.

Chapter Twelve

Kit knew before she'd ever opened her eyes the day was going to be a train wreck. When she'd reached out and found nothing but cool, empty space surrounding her, Kit knew there had been some sort of problem because that was the only reason she'd be alone. Another one of the perks of having two mates was that they made sure she never went to sleep alone, and certainly she never woke up alone—unless there was a problem that required both of them. Wishing she could just pull the pillow over her head and block out whatever was coming, Kit groaned when she heard the bedroom door open. "If you aren't here to set my body on fire again, go away."

Trev's chuckle filled the distance between them, "Sorry, baby, I promise we'll play with matches as soon as we can. But we need you downstairs, bright eyed and bushytailed in half an hour, so you need to get a move on." When she didn't move, Trev landed a sharp swat to the center of her ass causing her to jump from the bed spewing curses about his parents' marital status at the time of his birth. As she made her way to their large bathroom she saw him disappear into her closet and cringed. If he was laying out her clothes for her, then there really was something big going on and he was making sure she wouldn't be late. *Great, just fairy flippin' great.*

Kit felt as though she'd been through one of those assembly lines she'd seen on *The Jetsons*—where George was popped out of bed like a piece of toast and then scrubbed from head to toe before being dressed in a flash of robotic wonder before being thrust out into the world. Damn, she really shouldn't have spent all those Saturday mornings watching cartoons as a kid. When she opened the door to her mates' office, her second mug of coffee in hand, she froze when she saw the number of people already seated around the large room. A flare of panic moved through her and she frantically sought out her parents and grandmother before whispering, "Where are Ryan and Adana? Are they alright?"

Trev's warm arm came around her as he spoke, "They are fine, baby. No one has been hurt. This is about a rather significant security breach—I'm sorry I didn't explain that upstairs. We didn't mean to scare you. Please sit down, you need to hear what Devin has to say."

Kit's attention jerked to where Devin sat in front of Jameson's desk. Holy hell, how had she failed to notice him? The shit must have really hit the fan if the wizard they'd been so worried about bringing into the mansion was sitting in her mates' office sipping from a large mug of steaming tea. As she approached, he set the mug aside and stood, "Good morning, Kit. I'm sorry to interrupt your morning, but I'm afraid this couldn't wait." She spent the next hour listening as Devin related what he'd seen and heard outside the seal his brother was locked behind as well as his conversation with his brother. Kit knew Devin was taking a huge risk by coming to the estate without knowing who else might be working with his brother and she appreciated the fact he'd taken the chance because he was worried about Damian's increasingly erratic behavior. It hadn't taken long for the young witch to be identified,

Nick Michaels was immediately dispatched to her living quarters to bring her in and Jameson had assured the Supreme Council they would be able to take her as soon as he and Trev had an opportunity to speak with her alone. Kit cringed knowing the young woman was in for a tough lesson in the importance of pack loyalty.

By the time Devin had finished relating the events of the previous evening, Kit was trembling and she wasn't sure whether it was from paralyzing fear, blinding anger, a deep sense of betrayal, or some combination of all three. She was grateful Nick had secluded the young woman in a small room across the hall from the office, because Kit wasn't convinced she'd be able to rein in her temper, and evaporating the woman who had betrayed the pack that was every bit as important to her as her own family was certainly on her short list of options. Candles around the perimeter of the room were already starting to spark to flame, it was definitely time for her to step outside and dispel some of the energy swirling around inside her.

🐾 🐾 🐾

JAMESON LEANED BACK in his enormous leather chair and listened to Devin explain the rapidly escalating problem he believed his brother was becoming. The only time the wizard had seemed unsettled was when Marcus entered the room. The men might be half-brothers, but it was obvious they didn't know one another well. Jameson had studied Devin closely and was impressed he hadn't seen any hint of deception, nor had he caught that particular scent. One of the great things about being a shifter was the enhanced sense of smell—and something few people considered when they were trying to be deceptive was the fact their body's reaction to lying set off a chain reaction of chemical changes, and those changes were usually fairly easy for a shifter to pick up if they were paying attention. From all appearances, Devin was truly worried about his brother's potential to cause chaos and his words had clearly made an impression on the members of the Supreme Council who had joined them via a hastily established internet-meeting link.

'He's legit. And I think we've just gained an unlikely ally. I'm glad for a lot of reasons, but I'm particularly pleased that Kit's observations about the man have been validated.' Jameson agreed with Trev's comments and if the look on their sweet mate's face was any indication, she considered Devin a friend despite all of their warnings to remain cautious. *'I guess we should have met with him personally sooner, perhaps we could have saved ourselves a lot of groveling.'* And wasn't that the truth. For the first time in a long time, Jameson understood how humbling leadership could be. *'Don't you remember the dads telling us that this was how we'd know we were making progress? That anytime you are humbled you are learning?'* Jameson had struggled to hold back his chuckle, because he did indeed remember that particular lecture—and oddly enough, in this situation he found it comforting.

After the room cleared of everyone but Jameson, Trev, and Tristan, Nick led the young woman who had been working at the estate for the past several months into the room. They had known she was a magical, but her references had checked out so they'd hired her as part of the household staff. And now, in hindsight, it terrified him to think about how much access she'd had to his family. Jameson was sure Tristan and Nick were every bit as angry as he and Trev were, but they seemed to be holding their feelings in check—at least for the moment.

Jameson looked across his desk at the young woman who'd been seated across from him and knew they weren't going to get anything useful from the conversation. Everything about her had transformed right in front of his eyes. Gone was the mousey twenty-year-old he'd hired and in her place was a defiant woman without enough good sense to know she was sinking quickly in a cesspool of her own making. Jameson wasn't sure what the Supreme Council had planned for her and frankly, he didn't really give a rat's ass, but some of the things he'd heard mentioned didn't sound entirely pleasant. Evidently the Council had a special facility for what was called "re-programming" and even though he didn't know the details, the pinched expressions on the older magicals faces had given him the impression it wasn't going to be a pleasant experience for her.

The more defiant her body language became the angrier Jameson felt himself becoming. If he wasn't careful, he wasn't going to be in such a rage there wouldn't be anything left of her after this interview. Taking a deep breath, he leveled a look at her and saw a small flicker of fear in her dark eyes. *Good. She has good reason to be wary of me. I'd just as soon tear her limb from limb as look at her. There's a good reason wolves kill those who betray the pack.*

"Do you know why you are here, Pamela?" The woman sitting in front of him shuttered her expression and her total lack of emotion sent a chill through him. She looked at him with such disinterest, he wondered if she cared about anything but herself.

"Mr. Wolf, I'm not going to play games with you. If you have something to ask me, I suggest you just get to it, because I'm quite sure I'm being relieved of my duties here and I need to pack." *Fuck me, what an ice cold bitch. And if she thinks she is walking out of here to set up another scheme she can think again.*

"Check the attitude. I'm already walking a fine edge here. There isn't much holding my wolf back at this point." Jameson was confident that the implied threat was clear enough and took a perverse pleasure from the fact she paled significantly. "Tell us how you managed to join forces with one of the darkest wizards to ever live? And more importantly, what the fuck were you thinking targeting a member of our pack? Did you think helping Damian use a member of our family to lure in our mate would go unpunished?" By the time he'd finished his voice was practically a growl and he could feel the need to shift crashing over him in waves to rival a tsunami.

🐾 🐾 🐾

In his entire life, Trevlon Wolf hadn't seen his brother as close to losing control as he was now. He watched his twin struggle to hold his change back and he could feel the battle waging within him. Trev was also angry with the woman responsible for Angie's kidnapping, but as the senior Alpha, Jameson was taking on more of the blame for not protecting those around him—and Trev knew it was a very bitter pill to swallow. *'If you kill her, we'll never find out who else is involved.'*

'I'm trying. Really fucking trying. But she's hurt two of the most important women in my world—women who have never done a damned thing to her. She used Angie as a pawn—a fucking pawn. She didn't care a twit about the sweet woman Angie had grown into or all the children who depend on her. And that isn't even considering all those in the future who will benefit because they have somehow managed to cross Dr. Angie

Michaels' path.' Jameson took a deep breath and refocused on Pam Wing. "Who else in our employ knows what you were doing?" She just stared at him blankly without responding and Jameson didn't doubt that was how she'd respond to every question he asked, so he decided to save himself the effort and aggravation.

Turning to Tristan and Nick, he nodded, "She's all yours. Perhaps she'll be more inclined to answer your questions, quite frankly I don't give a flying fuck what condition she's in when you hand her over to the Supreme Council. After you search her room, please donate anything of value to a local charity and destroy the rest. If she thinks she can betray us without any consequences, she needs to learn differently." He turned his attention back to the traitor he'd just as soon take out as turn over to the magical community's governing body.

"As for you, until you learn the importance of honor and loyalty, stay away from our pack, our family, and our friends. You so much as breathe in a way that draws our attention and you'll find yourself facing a pack of angry wolves. It isn't a threat—it's a guarantee. There won't be a corner dark enough for you to hide in. We *will* find you." With that, he stalked from the room with Trev right behind him. He doubted the woman was going to be nearly as smug after the Michaels brothers finished with her—but frankly he just didn't care.

Chapter Thirteen

Kit had known when she woke up alone things were not right in her world, but she'd be damned if she's ever dreamed things had spiraled this far out of control. How had things gotten this screwed up in just a few short hours? The fact Damian had managed to get help on the inside of the estate terrified her, and Kit hated the fact she now looked at everyone around her with a measure of suspicion. "Damn, I really need more coffee if I'm going to get through this without going postal." Braden's snorted laugh sounded from beside her, letting Kit know she'd spoken aloud. He waved his hand dismissively and her cup filled with the steaming chocolate coffee mix he knew she favored and she couldn't hold back her own chuckle.

Braden's magic was quickly becoming so second nature to him that he often didn't even realize he'd was using magic to accomplish simple tasks. Kit was certain that Cecil's influence had helped the young man realize his upcoming role in the magic world, and she thanked the Universe for the older wizard mentorship of the teen. There were so many negative influences in the world and Braden had been exposed to so many of those he could have easily turned his back on everything he was destined to become. Just as she started to tell him how proud she was of the man he was becoming Jameson stalked through the room headed to the backdoor, his face contorted with a rage she'd never seen before and she unconsciously took a step to the side.

Jameson hit the doors with such force she worried they'd tear from their hinges before she saw his clothing shredding around him. She watched in fascination as he leapt from the large deck and shifted in mid-air. The remnants of his ripped clothing fluttered to the ground seconds after he'd already landed on the grassy turf at a dead run. She stood frozen in place, her mind spinning with questions. In all their time together, Jameson had never moved through a room where she was standing without at the very least acknowledging her, and it was highly unusual for him to have been this close and not touch her. In that moment, Kit realized how spoiled she'd become—how much she'd taken that attention for granted. Just as her breath caught, she felt Trev's arms come around her, "No, baby, this wasn't about you—well, not directly."

Turning in his arms, she tilted her head back to look up at him, "What does that mean? He looked mad enough to take a bite out of granite? I swear the entire house rocked on its foundation from his fury." Even as she spoke the words something in the back of her mind flickered to life.

"Oh he's pissed alright. Hell, I don't think I've ever seen him that close to completely losing it. But, baby, he isn't pissed *at you*, he's pissed *for you*. Well, for you and all the other members of our pack that he feels he's let down because he allowed that woman into our home. She was the first non-shifter we'd ever hired and knowing her deception allowed Angie to be taken is tearing him up inside." When Kit started struggling to free herself from his embrace, he tightened his arms around her like steel bands. She wanted to follow her mate, assure him that none of this was his fault. Hell, none of them had expected Damian to strike at a collateral target. Kit had been so confident Damian would come after her that she'd focused far too much of her training into fighting him face to face—a mistake she intended to correct immediately.

Trev's lips brushed over her temple before he spoke, "No, baby, let Jameson run it off. He needs this. Running is how he expends the negative energy that's feeding his anger. He'll need you more when he returns." Kit felt herself melt. *Damn it all to dimwitted demons anyway.* She felt him laugh against her and, try as she might, she couldn't hold back her own laughter. "The way your mind works fascinates me, baby. The sheer randomness of it is awe-inspiring."

"Says you—it drove my mother to distraction, although I must admit, it amused the hell out of my grandfather." A wave of loneliness crashed over her so suddenly she felt as if it had hit her like a coward's bullet, piercing her from the back, sending a crashing wall of cold water into her that threatened to pull her out into the sea of despair she'd nearly drowned in when her grandfather had first died. Her grandfather had been her rock, the solid place she'd always been able to anchor herself to during the turbulent storms that had come too frequently in their household when she'd been a child. Again, something in the back of her mind kindled with a spark of recognition, almost as if she was missing something that was painfully obvious before it flickered back to darkness.

Gripping her shoulders, Trev pushed her back to arm's length and studied her so closely she started to squirm under the scrutiny. There were storm clouds in his eyes and she was bewildered by the sudden change in him. Giving her a small shake, he barked, "Tell me. What was that?"

"What was what? Trevlon, I have no idea what you are talking about."

"The thought you just had. I saw it. The earth was shaking and boulders were tumbling all around you, but you weren't moving. It was if they were falling right through you." Kit could feel his rising panic and if she hadn't been concentrating on his emotions she might have wondered more at his strange words.

"I don't know what you are talking about. I had a fleeting thought of the loneliness I experienced on occasion as a child and then storms but then nothing after that." She felt her brow wrinkle as she fought to pull back the moment, to find out what kept dancing at the edge of her consciousness, but it was just beyond her grasp.

"Kit, over the past few days you've thought about rocks or something like that several times, often enough that even I have noticed and wondered what it meant." Braden's voice sounded concerned from beside her and she jerked her attention to the young man who seemed like such a kid in one moment and then so very wise beyond his years the next. He shrugged and started recalling several instances and as soon as he began, Kit saw a flash of the vision Trev had just described.

Clutching Brandon's arm with one hand and Trev's with the other, she felt herself sway with the enormity of what just flashed through her mind. The seal Damian was locked behind had been across the cave from where she'd been standing. Even though it hadn't been that far away, to her it looked as if she was looking through water. There were several witches and wizards standing in a semi-circle around the seal chanting, but Kit didn't understand the words. She'd had the impression they were younger and remembered having a fleeting thought wondering who'd taught the young men and women standing before her Latin. The only other time she'd heard it used was the day she and her mother had stood back and listened to the members of the Council speaking to her grandmother. But as she thought about it, the words didn't have the same sounds, so what were they speaking? Sanskrit? It was the only other language Kit knew was used by magicals when they were chanting from the most ancient texts.

She'd been able to hear Damian raging on the other side for them to hurry and then as if he'd known she was there he called out to her, pleading for her help. His voice modulated and became almost hypnotizing, reminding her of the Bible story about the serpent tempting Eve. His words whispered in her mind—imploring her to help, assuring her that all she had to do was concentrate and the seal would unlock. He'd told her others were getting close, but she could show them who held the real power. Even though she felt oddly disconnected from the scene, Kit felt the temptation of dark magic seeping clear to the depths of her soul. It would be so easy to show them how powerful she could be—the power that she only played with when no one was watching. The all-consuming power that seemed to call her more and more often into the meadow when everyone else was busy.

Trev's voice sounded so far away, but his pleading words finally broke through and Kit blinked up at him. She'd never seen such stark terror reflected in anyone's eyes as she did her mate's. Kit simply blinked up at his for several seconds wondering why he was so shaken. *It was just a daydream, it didn't mean anything—did it?* His voice once again broke through, the tone sharp, "It wasn't a dream, Kit. It was a fucking vision."

Trev felt as if his entire world had just shifted on its axis. His mother had often predicted her magic would flow through him one day, but he'd always assumed she was speaking metaphorically. But she had insisted that their mate would pull pieces of her magic from deep within him. Never one to back down, their mom had sworn Jameson was destined to become the alpha the prophets had been expecting for several hundred years. She had insisted her first-born son would lead their pack into a future that was sure to see their numbers increase exponentially and expand their influence to the world stage. And she'd repeatedly promised Trev he would find the magic that she'd blessed him with at birth.

As he'd held Kit's shoulders, connecting to what she was seeing and feeling, his mother's words had whispered through his mind. Was this the *gift* she'd promised? Seeing into the mind of someone else? Or seeing the future when it terrified him? What the hell kind of gift was that? *A gift I'd happily give up—that's for damned sure.* Why hadn't she given him something useful like the ability to see the numbers of the next lottery draw, or the ability to convince his mate to take care of herself? Yes, indeed, that would have been a gift worth having. But seeing what the future held when it was so weird he hadn't been able to fully unravel the images was fucking terrifying.

Trev kept his hands over the outside of her shoulders as he struggled to regain some semblance of control over his racing heart. Hell, he was practically panting at the fear that had stolen over his senses as he'd watched her tuck herself into the dark recesses of the cave. She'd stood back watching as the men and women surrounding some sort of symbol on the wall continued chanting. He hadn't understood their words, but when he'd seen the edges of the large golden symbol start to shimmer, he'd felt her torment. She'd been torn between helping and stopping them, but it had been the shaking of the earth around them that had really frightened him. When the boulders started falling all around them he'd screamed at her to run, but she had acted as though she couldn't hear him.

And now, she stood in front of him trembling and frightened at what she'd seen and he could feel her pulling back from him, "Baby, stay right where you are. And keep that sharp mind of yours here as well." Before he'd taken his next breath, Trev put out a distress call to his brother and felt Jameson's panic as he made a sharp U-turn and began racing back to the mansion. Their mind link automatically snapped tightly closed excluding all others from the conversation, just as it had their entire lives. Anytime one of them was in danger or hurt, everything intensified and narrowed—blocking out everything but the two of them.

Anytime there had been a security threat to their pack, Jameson and Trev purposely included anyone who needed to be informed, but he'd always felt as if the connection was diluted if others were a part of the conversation. Then when Kit entered their lives, they'd made concerted efforts to include her as often as possible, but that wasn't an option now. The fact the communication link only included the two of them was a testament to the fact Jameson had understood the fear his twin was feeling.

Trev could almost feel the cracks forming in Kit's mind as it started to shatter, and this new vulnerability was what terrified him. Their tiny mate had always been a force to be reckoned with, she'd shunned even the faintest shadows of weakness. But right now her mind was spinning wildly out of control, reminding him of those little steel balls in the old pinball machines he and his brother had played as kids. Seeing that small silver ball bouncing wildly under the glass, lighting up the features, dinging loudly as it racked up points had always fascinated him. Scooping her up in his arms, he raced up the stairs toward their suite hoping the security of her own space would help bring her back from the edge. Knowing the woman he loved more than life itself, was struggling to regain her equilibrium, her thoughts mimicking that little bit of round steel—well, that just fucking sucked.

Chapter Fourteen

Jameson turned so sharply his claws actually dug into the turf throwing bits of sod and grass to the side from the force. He hadn't asked where his brother was because he would have been able to find either his twin or their mate anywhere on the planet just by following his heart. The same was true of their children, which he didn't doubt was going to cause the two little hellions no end of grief. He'd been running long and hard trying to expend the negative emotions that had nearly swamped him as he'd watched the flippant attitude of the traitor who had sat across from him in his office. Knowing he'd misplaced his trust in a woman who had so blatantly endangered each and every member of his pack had almost broken his control. Had she displayed any contrition at all, he might have found a measure of compassion, but her blatant disregard for anyone but herself was what almost cost her life.

He'd been nearing the edge of their property when he'd heard Trev's frantic message. It was his brother's tone that had really worried him. What he'd heard wasn't fear in a way that said his physical safety had been compromised, but a fear of something he absolutely didn't understand—and that was far more terrifying. By the time he bounded over the deck railing he'd already shifted and landed on two feet rather than four. Tristan handed him a pair of pants and he hit the back door with enough force to send it crashing into the wall. Tristan's voice sounded behind him, "The Council had assured us the woman they escorted out of here will never return. My guess is she won't live much past her usefulness to them. And—" Jameson stopped when he heard the uncertainty in his friend's voice. Tristan Michaels had been the head of their security for years and his instincts were phenomenal. If Tristan sensed trouble, you could bet your ass there was problem that shouldn't be discounted or ignored.

"What?" Jameson hadn't intended for the question to sound as harsh as it had come out, but his patience was wearing thin—dangerously thin.

"Well, something about the Council members that came for the girl didn't seem quite right. I'd like to discuss it with all three of you as soon as possible. I'm also calling Ruby and Cecil." Tristan turned on his heel and headed for his office but called back over his shoulder, "Go check on your brother and mate. Something had shaken Trev up pretty bad."

Jameson didn't take time to respond, he just took off up the stairs, clearing them two and three at a time until he'd reached the second floor. It was a short sprint to the door of their suite and he was relieved to find Trev sitting in front of the black onyx fireplace with Kit curled up on his lap. *She just nodded off, but she won't stay asleep long when she senses you are here.* He'd no sooner heard Trev's words than Kit launched herself out of his brother's lap and into his arms. His fatigue evaporated the moment his arms locked around her securing her against his chest. Their heartbeats synchronized and Jameson felt a sense of peace roll through him just holding his mate against his bare chest. There was no denying the tension coming off his brother in waves, but Jameson intended to hold Kit against him for just a few precious seconds before delving into whatever had taken place after he'd left the house.

"My love, what happened?"

Trev shot to his feet and began pacing the width of the room with a restlessness Jameson couldn't remember having ever seen in his usually laissez-faire brother. Whatever had happened was obviously affecting Trev far more than Kit and that alone was worrisome. But Trev's stride was eating up the distance between the sitting room's floor to ceiling windows and the door faster on each pass—hell, he was practically vibrating with an energy that Jameson couldn't identify. His brother had rarely locked the door on their mind link, but it was sealed tight now.

"I had a little day dream—well, to be fair it was probably a little more than that, but Trev saw it too for some reason." She buried her face against his neck and Jameson took a moment to relish the feeling of her warm breath as it washed over his sweat damped skin. Ordinarily he'd have taken a quick shower before coming upstairs, but he hadn't wanted to waste those precious minutes. Any hesitance he'd had about skipping it dissolved in that instant, but then when she drew her tongue up in a slow lick, from the hallow above his collarbone to just below his ear, he felt blood surge to his cock tightening it to the point the skin was stretched painfully taunt. Damn, the woman could steal his focus faster than anything ever had.

"Goddammit, kitten. I know what you're doing and fuck me if it isn't working." He felt her shutter in his arms and knew he could be inside her in ten seconds—and it was too tempting so he loosened his arms and let her slowly slide to her feet. "Let's sort this out first, and then we'll pick up where we just left off—I promise." Her groan at the loss of physical contact vibrated clear to his soul, tempting him to reverse his decision, but one look at his brother let him know he'd made the right call.

Just as Kit started to recount what she'd seen, there was a thunderous knock on the door. Hell, Jameson had even startled at the booming sound of someone's fist battering against the thick wooden door. He didn't get a chance to ask who it was before Nick Michaels' voice sounded from the other side. "It's Nick. I have Braden with me. You need to hear what he has to say." That was one of the things Jameson loved about Nick—the man couldn't be any more direct in his communication. But even though he admired the man there were times when his timing really sucked. He opened the door and ushered them in, then excused himself to pull on a shirt because it was hard telling who else was going to show up.

Jameson spent the next hour listening to three versions of the same story—each one similar, but still unique in their perspective. Trev's anxiety was certainly easy to understand. They'd both wondered hundreds of times about the meaning of their mother's cryptic promise about what Trev's gift would be. She and their dads hadn't been at all ambiguous when they'd explained what gifts he'd been given, but explanations about Trev's gift had always been remarkably vague. Up to this point, neither of them had ever exhibited any magical abilities, so Jameson understood Trev wasn't just upset about what he'd seen. Jameson fully understood his brother's trepidation because this was a game changing moment. Hell, they'd shared everything from the womb and for the first time, Trevlon had experienced something that had Jameson hadn't even sensed.

"I was thinking." Braden hadn't said much after his initial description of what he'd seen. He simply sat quietly next to Nick and listened to Kit and Trev's versions. Turning to Kit, he asked, "Did you notice that you weren't seeing things very clearly? Like you were looking through water?" She looked surprised, but nodded. He smiled then and continued, "I think you weren't really there—well, not your actual body. Geez, I'm not saying this right. I think you and I projected you there, sort of like a hologram."

When Braden paused, Nick nudged him, "Tell them. This is no time to decide to be shy. Hell, I thought we'd gotten past this point, son." It warmed Jameson's heart to hear Nick's endearment for the young wizard. When Braden had first arrived at the estate, he'd almost been traumatized by years of being on the run. When Damian hadn't been able to acquire his grandson by the time the young man approached the age he'd come into his full powers, the dark wizard decided to kill him. Luckily Carla Harris had been nearby and managed to rescue Braden. With mere moments to spare, Carla had whisked Braden off to the hospital where Angie Wolf-Michaels had been working. Angie had assured them that Carla's swift actions had been the only thing that kept Damian from being successful.

"Yes, sir." Braden took a deep breath and then leaned forward meeting Kit's gaze, "I think you and I joined our power to send you there. Well, I mean, I think we could do it. I'm not sure it was so much a vision as a message. Like someone on the other side was saying *here,* 'This is how you can do this' if you know what I mean. I think you can go and see who is helping him without *really being there.* But you'll have to be careful because they'll be able to see you just like Trev did."

Jameson watched as Kit unfolded her legs from beneath her, standing quickly before she began pacing the same path Trev had been using earlier. He hid his smile but wondered what it would look like if they all three paced like that to help them focus and think—hell, it would look like something akin to the Chinese fire drills they'd done as kids whenever they stopped at stop signs—God that had driven their parents to distraction.

Braden tilted his head to the side and looked at Jameson thoughtfully, "You ran around the car at stop signs? Why?" *Fuck me, this kid is so smart he's dangerous.*

This time Jameson couldn't hold back his laughter, "I promise to teach you." Then he leaned closer to whisper conspiratorially, "It'll drive your parents insane—so it's well worth the effort." He couldn't help but smile at Nick's growled threats of retribution—times two.

🐾 🐾 🐾

KIT PACED BACK and forth letting her mind work through everything. She wasn't listening to the chatter around her, she'd discovered that was one of the great things about having small children—she'd had to learn how to tune out unnecessary distractions. There was still a piece of the puzzle missing, one she instinctively knew she had to have before they took any action. There was something missing, turning to Trev she interrupted the nonsense happening around her to ask, "Downstairs you said something about tumbling boulders—what was that?"

Her mate closed his eyes and she watched as his expression became tortured, and when he opened his eyes and met her gaze, the fear that reflected in his dark eyes caused her to suck in a quick gasp. She'd known he had been shaken to his core by what he'd seen, but in truth Kit had been so absorbed in trying to sort out her own feelings she hadn't really taken time to consider what her mate was going through. Chastising herself for her selfishness, Kit moved quickly so she was standing directly in front of Trev. Taking his hands in hers, she leaned forward and pressed her lips softly against the side of his neck whispering, "I'm sorry."

Trev pulled back, studying her with his brow raised in question so Kit continued, "I knew you were upset, but I didn't take time to hear you out. That isn't what mates are supposed to do. It certainly wasn't loving, nor was it even fair." His eyes softened and he pulled her into his arms, and for the first time since they'd come upstairs, Kit felt as if they were finally set on a path to resolve their problem with Damian.

Turning her so she was standing beside her, Trev pulled her tightly against his side before speaking to the group, "Part of my disquiet about what happened downstairs is related to something personal that my mother said before she died—but I'm going to leave that out of this particular discussion. What is important here is the part Kit just mentioned. I saw huge rocks and gigantic boulders falling all around her. I could still see the seal and hear the chanting she and Braden have mentioned but not the people. My initial fear was that I was seeing the love of my life buried alive, but after listening to Kit and Braden, I agree that she wasn't a solid form." Kit realized now that he'd been terrified that he was seeing her death, and she couldn't help turning to wrap her arms around his waist. After what had happened to their parents, he had to have been horrified by what he'd seen.

Tightening her arms around him, Kit was once again

humbled by how much more she received than she gave in her relationship with her mates. Knowing the depth of his fear for her was just one more example of their remarkable capacity for unconditional love. As the discussion continued to swirl around them the room began filling up until Jameson's deep voice finally boomed over everyone, "Let's adjourn this for now. Everyone meet in the downstairs meeting room first thing tomorrow morning—and I do mean everyone. Any pack member who is free, needs to be there. Nick, make sure everyone is notified and I'd certainly like to see Kit's family and Cecil there as well. It's time to get a plan in place and wrap this thing up."

Kit couldn't have agreed more. She was tired of living with the entire mess hanging over her head. The dark wizard was taking up entirely too much time in her life and Kit was more than ready to relegate him to her past.

🐾 🐾 🐾

LIBBY WELLS WAS physically and emotionally exhausted. She'd spent months working sixteen hour days and now that the project was completed, her research all compiled and her presentation nearly ready. She already felt lost, oddly adrift, and technically she wasn't even finished yet. She still needed to make the trip to the convention and present her findings. She had taken time this evening to go down the street to the small deli for a sandwich; after Charlie's admonishment about how much weight she'd lost, Libby had tried to be more conscious of taking care of herself.

The night she had spent with the two shifters had reminded her that there really was more to life than work. Holy shit those two had set her entire body on fire from their first touch. She'd heard Kit and her friends talking about all the benefits of ménage relationships, but she'd honestly thought they were exaggerating when they'd spoken about the pleasure—*not!* The two men had made love to her all night and oddly enough the next morning she'd been totally energized rather than exhausted. They had both smiled and assured her that her observation was precisely what they'd wanted her to see, and then proceeded to make her promise to call them as soon as she returned to the city.

Before she'd gotten in her car the next morning, Libby had blurted out the question that had haunted her since she'd arrived the afternoon before. When she'd asked the men if they'd been watching her, they had both tilted their heads to the side in question before hustling her back inside the mansion. After she'd explained she'd had the strangest feeling she was being watched, they'd given her a small caliber pistol and made sure she knew exactly how to use it. Both men had also promised to accompany her to the convention and begun making the arrangements.

Libby had barely had a moment to herself since. Either Charlie or Dirk had been at her side almost every moment since, and it was only this afternoon that she'd convinced them she would be fine until they all met at the airport tomorrow morning. Now, walking down the deserted hallway leading to her office, Libby knew she'd made a huge mistake.

Standing in the hallway outside her office at the university, she felt the fine hairs at the back of her neck stand up on end. Reaching into her bag as if she were looking for her keys, Libby wrapped her fingers around the small pistol they'd given her and flipped off the safety—cringing at how loud the click had sounded. When she turned around, she faced the ugliest creature she'd ever seen. The first thing she noticed was that she couldn't tell if it was male or female. The long black robe was tattered and torn with what looked like burned holes scattered over the surface. But it was the black sword that held her attention, when the creature raised the weapon overhead, Libby didn't hesitate—she fired her own weapon, emptying the small clip. Watching in horror as the body dropped to the floor, Libby felt her knees go out from under her. As she slid to the floor, she was barely aware of shouting and the clamor of heavy footsteps as people raced to her side.

Chapter Fifteen

Kit felt the pleasure building until her head fell back against the pillow and colorful sparkles of light began dancing behind her eyelids, "Open those beautiful green eyes, kitten. I want to see your need. You pleasure belongs to us—don't deny us the chance to see it...to hear it." She was certain it would be much easier to fight back the pleasure and open her eyes if he would stop using the tip of his tongue to draw circles around her clit. Goddess, the man was absolutely ruthless at times.

"If you'd just fuck me already, I'd be more inclined to behave." She was drowning in the endorphins flooding her system so she didn't care how pathetically needy she'd sounded. All those feel good chemicals racing through her system were just a preview of coming attractions and she was more than a little anxious to get to the main event. Her body was gearing up for her coming heat—she could feel it, and the primal need to mate was tightening its hold on her with each passing minute. Perhaps she was using it as an excuse for her behavior, but she didn't care—she was horny and fully intended to be sated...and sooner rather than later. Was it horrible that she was so unrepentant? Hell, she didn't even care about that.

"You are awfully demanding for a sub, baby. What makes you think we'll just give in to you?" Trev's voice was soft and entreating despite the words he'd spoken. He didn't fool her for a minute. He was going to give her everything she was demanding and more. He'd never been the demanding Master that Jameson was, though the two of them did a bang up job of playing good cop bad cop if you asked her.

Just as she opened her mouth to speak Jameson's palm landed a stinging swat to her ass. "I think you've made enough demands, sweet sub. Let's see if you can manage to earn some of the satisfaction you seem to think you deserve." Jameson's words were more direct and she knew he thought he was intimidating, but his eyes were gleaming with lust and Kit fully intended to play that for all it was worth.

"What do you want me to do, Sir? You know there is nothing I won't do for you—both of you, don't you?" She'd tried for sweet, but the grins on their faces told her neither of them were buying it. "What?"

"Baby, you are just about the worst liar who ever walked the face of the earth. And just in case you think that's an insult—think again, because it's actually one of the many things we love about you. Well, that and your brilliant mind and your lovely ass." Trev's smile was pure devilment and she had to fight the urge to roll her eyes at him. "Oh, baby, rolling your eyes would indeed be a very bad idea." *Damn I really hate it when they do that.*

"I don't know what you mean. I didn't roll my eyes at you, Sir. I'd never do anything that disrespectful." Kit even batted her eyes to add to the effect that she was really trying to behave—but both of her mates burst out laughing. Maybe it was the hormones building up as her body readied itself for mating, but she felt tears fill her eyes. It didn't make any sense that her feelings were hurt, hell— she knew they were just teasing her, but still.

"Oh, kitten, we fully intend to take care of you. We weren't trying to upset you and we should have known better—you're far too close to your heat to tolerate our teasing." Jameson's words soothed her, but it was the feel of his calloused fingers trailing a line of fire up her arm that flipped the moment back to sensual. Goddess above the two of them could set her entire soul on fire so easily it was almost embarrassing—*almost*. "You are our mate, kitten. The other half of our souls. There isn't anything we wouldn't do for you—well, except let you go. We'll never let you go. You own us—you know that, right? We belong to you just as you belong to us."

It was true. Kit knew it to the depths of her soul. They belonged to her heart and soul—now she just wanted them to get their cocks inside her and prove it. Oh yeah, her heat was no longer creeping up on her, it was now in a full frontal charge. In the back of her mind, Kit hoped the problem with Damian could be resolved quickly because she knew all too well how consuming the need to fuck was once she was fully in season. Most wolf shifters rarely left their beds during that time. Hell, they didn't care about much except the mindless pursuit of their next orgasm. Sex with Jameson and Trev was always mind-blowing, but there was always a sense of urgency during her heat that ramped everything up to the point it was an all-consuming obsession. A mindless need that only her mates could satisfy.

The more aroused she became, the more it spurred her mates' desire and at the present rate, Kit figured they were all three going to erupt into a ball of scorching flames within minutes. "Perhaps you should give our sweet sub something else to think about besides her need to come, brother. Her greedy little body seems very focused on one particular goal, and I for one am not ready for this to end just yet." Jameson's growled words vibrated over her bare sex sending another wave of her cream rushing down the channel to slide over the bare, swollen lips of her sex. "Oh, sweetheart, that rush of your sweet syrup is exactly what I've been waiting for. You taste like a summer night in the meadow during a spring rain—and it's the most addictive drug in the world. But nothing changes the fact that no matter how intense the need building in my groin is—it will always be surpassed by the love in my heart."

Kit was listening—mostly. But the feel of the engorged head of Trev's cock pressing between her lips to slide over her tongue was quickly stealing her concentration. She could still feel Jameson's tongue lapping through the folds of her sex, the closer their wolves pressed to the surface the rougher their tongues became until just the smallest contact would be enough to push her over the top. But he was right, she didn't want this to end just yet either. When the engorged head of Trev's cock pressed against her lips, Kit felt the liquid silk of his pre-cum. His harsh growl of satisfaction as he painted her lips with the pearly drops drove her own desperation even higher. She parted her lips just enough for him to push his way in because she knew both of her mates loved the feeling of power they got from shoving their way in on the first pass.

"Fuck! That is amazing, baby. Your mouth feels like a plunge into hot, wet silk. Holy Goddess save me from the rapture of your tongue. You are going to steal my control far too quickly if you keep that up." Kit was wrapping her tongue around his cock as he slid in and out in ever deepening thrusts. She paid particular attention to the sensitive spot just under the rim of his bulbous head and wanted to smile at the animalistic growls coming from deep in his throat. "Brother, you need to step it up or she's going to suck the cum right out of my balls and I'm not going to be able to hold anything back from her. Our woman's mouth is fucking lethal."

🐾 🐾 🐾

JAMESON COULDN'T TAKE his eyes off the scene playing out in front of him. Kit was spiraling out of control faster than any other time since her last cycle and it was the hottest thing he'd ever seen. The longer they were mated they more sexually attracted he was to the sweet witch whose bare sex he was tongue fucking. And if you had asked him the first night he'd met her, Jameson would have sworn things couldn't get any hotter. For years Jameson had heard Doms at the clubs they'd frequented complain endlessly about their subs "losing their sexual appeal". Since shifters mate for life, it had been a niggling concern in the back of his mind for years. Just thinking about spending the rest of his life with someone he didn't find sexually attractive, someone whose sole appeal was the fact she belonged to him hadn't set well at all.

Jameson had always hoped the mate who had eluded them so long would appeal to both he and his brother, but even in his wildest dreams he hadn't envisioned the sexual attraction they both felt with Kit. Every time they fucked her it was better than the time before, and knowing she was coming into season just meant things would be escalating in a big way and soon. In the back of his mind, Jameson considered how dangerous it would be for them to be too distracted by the problems with Damian—if things weren't resolved soon they'd need to turn things over to their Betas. And even though he knew Tristan and

Nick were more than capable of tackling the problem, Jameson knew they were still monitoring Angie closely after her kidnapping. For now, he pushed the concerns to the back of his mind. Worry didn't have any place in their bedroom—not when his wolf was pressing at him and he could feel his tongue elongating and roughing as he lapped at Kit's labia.

The scent of his mate drove him to distraction—plain and simple. The difference in her fragrance as her body readied itself for the intensity of their sexual exploits while she was in heat fascinated him. Her cream took on a much earthier scent and thickened to protect her delicate tissues from the rigors of their insatiable hunger. The liquid silk sliding over his tongue in sweet rivulets would become as thick as maple syrup in the winter during the next few days and he nor Trev would be able to get enough of it.

"Kitten, your pussy is as sweet and juicy as a ripe peach. And feeling the walls of your channel quiver as those greedy muscles try to pull my tongue deeper is making me insane with the need to fuck you." He let the words settle for a few seconds before he continued, "But you know the rules, my love—you have to come before we'll give you what we all want." He and Trev wouldn't take her together until she'd already had at least one release. They never wanted to push her to physically accept them before she was ready, and their sexy little mate tended to think she was ready long before they did. Jameson had heard horror stories from other shifters about torn tissues and ruptures, hell, he had nightmares about hurting Kit.

"Please, oh please. I'm going to die if I don't have you." Her voice was thin and raspy with need. *'Perfect. Just the way we want her. Let's do this, brother—before I explode.'*

Jameson met Trev's eyes and gave him an almost imperceptible nod, then watched as his brother cupped her cheek and began thrusting quicker and deeper each time he slid past her swollen lips. Goddess above the woman was beyond beautiful—inside and out—and he couldn't fucking wait to be inside her. Watching his brother strain to hold back his release, Jameson knew they needed to send her over the edge into bliss and then treat themselves to the pleasures only Kit could give them.

'Give her the command, man. I can see how close you are and you don't want to fuck up and miss the main event.' Trev barely let him finish the thought before he pulled back and growled, "Come for us, mate. Now." Jameson felt her entire body stiffen as if every muscles had locked down at precisely the same moment. Even though Trev had sealed his lips over hers, the muffled sound of her scream went straight to Jameson's cock and he nearly came against their smooth cotton sheets. Hell, he hadn't lost control of a release before he'd been inside a woman since he was a damned teenager. Cursing his body's lack of control, he shifted uncomfortably without ever slowing the pace of his tongue's thrusts.

Linking to Kit's mind was probably a mistake, but he couldn't help himself. Feeling her orgasm was almost as good as having one himself. The depth of her ecstasy was always humbling, but he wondered how much more intense it would be as she neared her cycle. Jameson felt the jolt as if he'd been hit with a high voltage line—hell, lightening probably wouldn't have packed a punch more powerful. He couldn't actually see what she was seeing, but he felt as he'd been run over by a bus when her emotions rolled over him. The pure ecstasy that she was feeling pounded into Jameson with so much force he felt his canines lengthen as his wolf pushed ever closer to the surface.

Jameson moved quickly into position as Trev lay back on the bed and pulled their still trembling mate on to his heaving chest. "Baby, you nearly gave me a heart attack. God, I need inside you. Now. Right fucking now." Jameson watched as Kit trembled and attempted to position herself over Trev, but she was obviously struggling to make her arms and legs cooperate. Hell, after what he'd felt from her, Jameson was impressed she was still conscious.

"Here, kitten, let me help you." When she was filled with his brother, Jameson watched Trev pull her down to his chest. "Let Trev love you, kitten. I'm going to make sure you are ready for me so we all enjoy this as much as possible. And baby, if we can make this even half as good as the orgasm you just shared with me—hell, I'll die a happy man."

Jameson used the time he spent massaging lube into the tight ring of muscles around Kit's rear entrance to rein in his raging drive to sink into her heat with pounding strokes that would rocket them both into orbit. But listening to Trev's sweet words of encouragement and feeling her relax into his touch gave him enough time to reflect on how truly blessed they were to have found such a perfect mate. Leaning forward, he nipped at each of the rounded globes of her ass before pulling them apart and positioning himself to slide into heaven.

"Are you ready for me, kitten?" Jameson could hear the roughened tone of his voice. Watching as her pupils dilated in response to his blatant question, he didn't wait for her response. "Fuck, you are already burning me alive and I've only pressed the tip of my very greedy cock against your heat." Taking a steadying breath, Jameson refocused his attention on controlling his desire to just power into her and letting his cock find its satisfaction without regard to Kit's pleasure.

Skimming his hands up the expanse of her back, Jameson marveled at the creamy skin that felt like warm satin beneath his hands. He and Trev hadn't been monks during the years they'd waited for Kit to find her way to them, but Jameson knew to the bottom of his soul that no woman had ever felt this perfect. Her skin was practically molten beneath his fingertips, hell, it was a wonder she didn't erupt into flames herself rather than setting the candles surrounding them ablaze. Skimming his palms over the rounded curves of her ass, Jameson continued preparing her with a special lube that would not only warm those sensitive tissues coaxing them to relax, but it would also provide her with the added sensation of a slow escalation of tingling. By the time he was stroking in and out of her tight little ass, Kit would feel like her entire sex was being caressed by a thousand tiny fingers all intent on maximizing her pleasure.

One of the things Kit had taught him was that he didn't need to control her sexually to be her Dom—he simply had to harness and direct the power that was already there. Providing her with opportunities to tune in to her innate sensuality was all that was required—once he or Trev accomplished that, they only needed to sit back and watch in wonder as she flowered into her sexuality right in front of their eyes.

Sinking deep into Kit's ass was one of the most erotic things Jameson had ever experienced. Hearing her panting beneath him, watching as a fine sheet of sweat broke out over her back, listening to each soft moan as she submitted herself completely to him—it was a symphony of pure erotic pleasure. *'Stop waxing fucking poetic and move. She is already quaking around my cock and I'm going to come before she gets hers if you don't get this show on the road.'* Trev's desperate plea wasn't a complete surprise. Hell, Jameson should have expected it because his brother had been inside their mate for several minutes and that alone was enough to send a sane man to the edge of reality.

Without any preamble Jameson gripped her hips as he leaned forward to whisper, "Hang on, kitten, this is going to be a fast roller coaster ride to heaven." He began pulling back and felt Trev's cock shifting on the other side of the thin membrane separating them. His brother was more than ready and they alternated their strokes to make sure Kit knew one of them was always possessing her—filling her. The lesson was as much emotional as physical—one of them would always be by her side. When her entire body started to shake, Jameson leaned down letting his wolf push to the surface just enough for his canines to elongate. He opened his mouth over the sensitive spot at the top of her shoulder where he had originally bitten her during their mating and let himself sink into her skin once again.

Chapter Sixteen

Kit's mind floated back to an old western she'd watched late one night and remembered hearing the expression 'ridden hard and put up wet'. At the time she had wondered what on earth the cowboy had meant, but as she tried to drag herself out from beneath Trev's heavy arm and scoot from the bed, she suddenly understood the expression all too clearly. She barely managed to hold back her moan as her muscles protested her bladder's demand for her to move. By the time she'd taken care of business and stepped into the steaming shower, she felt Trev's very naked and extremely aroused body press against her back, his arm snaking around her in a tight band just under her breasts. His warm breath moved over her neck and the minty smell let her know he'd probably gotten up as soon as she'd left the bed. Her men always knew the moment she wasn't within reach, it was one of the things she loved about them.

"Why are you out of bed, baby? I wanted to massage all your aches and pains away before you had to face the day."

"I need to work with Braden and Granny Good Witch today—see if I can't perfect that hologram technique." There was also something else she wanted to test, but she wasn't going to mention that part just yet. Sometime during the night, the small voice that had been trying to speak to her subconscious the past few days had finally managed to break through her dreams and she'd figured out exactly how to seal Damian behind the seal forever. She knew *how*, now all she had to do was find out if she could pull it off.

"I can practically feel your mind spinning, Kit. But first things first..." Trev moved her further into the steaming shower and positioned her under the large rainfall showerhead in the center of the large enclosure. Kit closed her eyes letting the warmth of the water seep into her tight muscles. The bites her mates had given her last night were healed but still tender, and Kit smiled when Trev's soaped hands skimmed lovingly over those spots. "I know they are still sensitive, baby, but damn we love reminding you that you belong to us." He washed her with a keen perception of all the places needing loving attention, and Kit felt herself sinking into a blissful state of relaxation that threatened to melt her into a puddle beneath his feet.

The scent of citrus and sage drifted around her as he washed her hair massaging her scalp until she actually swayed against him. "Hang on, baby, I'll take care of you." His soft promise was followed by him moving her to the large stone bench and rinsing the fragrant conditioner from her hair with one of the hand-held nozzles they'd installed when they'd remodeled the shower. Kit loved the one-way glass wall that let her look out over the expansive backyard of the estate, it gave her the feeling of showering in nature even when the winter weather made her want to snuggle in front of a warm fire.

Watching as Trev quickly cleaned himself, Kit couldn't help but admire him. He and Jameson held her heart, they gave all of themselves to her, but they rarely gave her the opportunity to simply look at them. She knew they were mirror image twins, but they had never looked *alike* to her, but perhaps it was just because she considered their energy signatures to be so very different. Watching Trev's tight abdominal muscles flex beneath his tanned skin as he washed his dark hair was making her mouth water with the need to outline each peak and valley with her tongue. The taste of their skin was different and Kit loved the fact she could tell them apart in the dark by just scenting or tasting them.

Kit felt her sex flooding as it prepared itself for her mate's possession, just watching the way he moved, the innate grace of a predator made her blood heat and was quickly setting her body on fire. When he stopped moving, Kit let her eyes travel slowly up until they met his. "Baby, you need to stop looking at me like that or we're not going to get out of the suite for hours—fuck, you'll be lucky to get out of the shower before noon." Before he'd even finished speaking she'd lowered herself to her hands and knees before slowly closing the distance between them. When she cupped his balls rolling them in her palm while her other hand stroked the heavily veined length of his cock she heard him groan, "Fuck me, baby. You're going to kill me." He felt like velvet covered steel and he was all hers. The power of that thought staggered her.

Enveloping the engorged head in her mouth, Kit head Trev's gasped, "Goddamn, baby. Your mouth should be registered as a fucking weapon." The rush of moisture to her sex filled the shower with her scent and Kit watched Trev's nostrils flare in recognition. "I know you are sore this morning, baby, so I'm not going to fuck you. I want to play a game, though. As you blow my mind, I'm going to fill yours with a play-by-play of how it feels—and I'm going to try to make you come just from my words alone." He moaned as she traced her tongue along the underside of his corona, "Do you want to play, love?"

Kit hummed her agreement knowing she was already on the fast track to climaxing just from the feel of him against her tongue. The more he filled her mouth with his taste the more excited she became. "That's feels so good, baby. Let a shadow of your wolf come out, your tongue will get longer and rougher—holy fuck, that's it, baby." Kit made a conscious effort to link her mind to his and gasped at the feelings that moved through her. She caught swirls of color and glimpses of erotic images she knew instantly were flashbacks from their time together playing in his mind like an X-rated home movie. "You own me. I always dreamed of finding a mate who I could love but, baby, you are so much more. You ignite a hunger in me that I didn't even know existed, and Goddess knows I had enough previous experience, I should have known it all."

His words might have ignited jealousy if she hadn't understood the deeper message behind them. Kit had avoided finding her mate because she hadn't wanted to give up her freedom, what she had never envisioned was the she would simply be trading one kind of freedom for another. Sure, her men could be bossy and unreasonable, but they gave her wings to fly simply because she was confident in the knowledge they would always catch her if she fell. Tightening her lips around his throbbing cock, Kit pushed him to the back of her throat and swallowed several times knowing exactly how that deep massage of her throat muscles would affect him.

Glancing up, Kit watched Trev's head fall back, his mouth open as he shouted her name. Tightening his hands in her hair, Trev's mind went spinning and his pleasure pulled her along with him as they both flew right over the edge into a ravine of pure rapture. Kit felt her entire body convulse as her own orgasm rocked her clear to the bottom of her being. The hot pulses of his seed coated the back of her throat and swallowing each powerful jet seemed to prolong his release. When he finally pulled from her mouth, Kit sighed at the loss. Holding him in her mouth had been intimate—a connection unlike any other and she shivered. His voice finally broke the silence and it was only then she realized he'd turned off the water. "Come. We need to get you dry and warmed up." Pulling her to her feet, he pulled a towel from the warming rack and blotted her hair before drying her quickly and wrapping her soft terry robe around her.

Cared for. Cherished. There wasn't any feeling in the world quite as comforting as knowing she was safe in her mates' care. They took far better care of her than she did of herself and she often wished she could thank their parents in person for raising such amazing sons. Before he let her go, Trev pulled her into his arms and just held her against his chest. "You are my heart, Kit. I love my brother. I adore my children. But, you are my heart. The terror I felt when I thought you were going to be buried alive in that deep cavern is something I never want to experience again."

Kit cuddled closer and let the plan she'd been working on continue to play out in her mind. If things worked as she hoped they would, none of them would have to worry about Damian for much longer.

Chapter Seventeen

Jameson stood in the shadows of the "lab" as they called the building they'd built for Kit as a safe place to practice her magic watching as she and Braden struggled to project the hologram as Ruby and Cecil coached them from the side. He hadn't mentioned Libby's scare at the university because he hadn't wanted to distract her, but he wouldn't be able to it keep it from her much longer. He'd dispatched Charlie and Dirk to move Libby to the estate as soon as his contact at the police department had alerted him. The weapon she'd used to kill the man who'd attacked her with a jewel-encrusted sword was registered to him, so he'd been notified almost immediately.

The detective who'd called had been a friend for many years and Jameson appreciated the fact he'd taken extra care to watch over Libby until Charlie and Dirk had gotten to her. The two younger men had been beside themselves for allowing her out of their sight—Jameson could totally relate to their frustration. He intended to make sure Kit's sweet friend was well protected until this was over, and then he'd sit back and watch as Charlie and Dirk learned what the other mated men in their pack already knew—keeping your woman safe was a full-time job.

Jameson refocused his attention on the four people standing in front of him. He knew Ruby and Cecil would be able to help when the time was right, but when he'd talked to the two older magicals earlier, they'd explained Kit and Braden needed to maximize their own abilities or nothing was going to work as planned. He had to admit, Kit's plan to find out who was in the semi-circle of hooded figures she'd seen was important, but personally he'd rather they just send shockwaves through the rocks and bury the fucker alive. Damian had been causing heartache around the world for generations and it was high time he was stopped—permanently.

"Have you tried touching her while she attempts this?" Jameson had sensed Marcus's presence at the estate, but was startled to find him standing so close. "You are a shifter, you are an earthbound creature. As magicals, Kit and Braden both draw energy from the earth, but they can't maintain the level of connection they need unless they are well grounded. You can provide that. It may take you and your brother together, as a matter of fact, I can almost assure you that it will—but the boost it will give them will be exactly what they are lacking."

Jameson turned to Marcus raising a brow in question. "How did you know what was going on here or do I even want to now?"

Marcus chuckled, "You probably don't, but I'll tell you anyway because I'm not sure you'll believe me and it lets me off the hook either way." There were times—like now—that Jameson really wasn't in the mood for Marcus's selfish bullshit, but he kept quiet. "Her grandfather asked me to help. Kit and Ruby are both so focused they aren't hearing his whispers to them." When Jameson just stared at him, Marcus smiled, "See, I knew you'd be skeptical—case in point for an earthbound creature. You believe what you see and question what you don't, even if it is just as true. And I'll remind you that you are part magical, so you could see the other dimensions of reality if you would just try."

He and Trev had suffered through more than one lecture from Marcus about their inability to "see" the other dimensions Marcus swore were right in front of them. When they'd been lost in their grief, their mentor had insisted that all they had to do was open their minds and they would be able to see their parents standing but a few feet in front of them. But they'd insisted there wasn't anything wrong with their eyesight and there was nothing but open space in front of them. Marcus Hines had always had a mystical attitude, but they hadn't known he was actually magical until recently. That discovery had gone a long way to explain some of their previous discussions with the man.

Marcus leaned forward and challenged, "What do you have to lose in trying? Ask them to step outside, remove your shoes and socks, and stand in the grass so you are as anchored as possible. Then place your hands on Kit's bare skin—preferably atop a chakra center. Step up behind her and place your hands beneath her shirt over her lower abdomen. When they begin again don't let go." *Don't let go? What the hell did that mean?* When he turned to ask for an explanation, Marcus was gone. *Damn, I hate it when he does that shit.*

By the time Jameson had finished explaining Marcus's instructions to Kit and Braden, Trev had joined them. He'd seen the sheen of tears in his sweet mate's eyes when he had mentioned her grandfather's failed attempts to whisper in her ear. Once they'd all moved outside, Jameson felt a sense of peace as he wiggled his bare toes down into the soft grass in front of Kit's lab. He and Trev stood in a V behind their mate so they could each slip a hand beneath her shirt and the waistband of her pants to rest their palms over her bare abdomen. The connection was instantaneous and Jameson marveled at the fact that he could almost feel a current of power pulsing between the three of them.

Ruby and Cecil stood to the side—watching and waiting, their faces filled with an odd look of tension Jameson didn't understand. *Why are they so concerned about what Kit and Braden are going to see?* Even before Trev had a chance to ask his silent question, Jameson remembered both Kit and Braden mentioning a semi-circle of people chanting in front of the seal. *Perhaps those people are the key.* After all, Damian wasn't a *real* threat as long as he was contained behind the magical seal. No leader—good or evil, has any *real* power without followers. And, Jameson was certain he remembered Devin mentioning something about Damian's followers growing in numbers.

Looking up, Jameson realized Devin had joined them and all three magicals were studying him. Cecil nodded his head in silent acknowledgement and Ruby grinned before waving her wrinkled hand above her head to briefly flash a colorful image of a shining light bulb. Jameson chuckled at her cartoon representation of someone who had just figured something out. His affection for Ruby continued to grow as did his respect for her. He couldn't hold back his feeling of loss as he wished his mother and fathers had lived to meet Kit. He often missed them for himself and his brother, but this was the first time he could honestly say he felt cheated out of being about to introduce his wife to them. Shaking his head to banish the melancholy he felt descending around him, Jameson flexed his fingers over Kit's bare skin and whispered against her ear, "Your body is already warming as it prepares itself for your heat. I can feel the energy building within you. Let's get this done so we can run in the moonlight tonight." He felt her tense beneath his touch and licked the shell of her ear, "Consider it a prelude."

🐾 🐾 🐾

KIT FOCUSED ALL of her energy on casting spell as she, Braden, and Devin chanted—the spell was supposed to send her spirit to the cavern that held the magical seal. That seal was the only thing separating Damian from the rest of the world—the seal Kit had unknowingly locked him behind when he'd intended to hurt Jameson and Trevlon. She still didn't know how she'd done it, all she knew was that her desire to protect her mates had her do something everything considered impossible.

As they'd promised, her grandmother and Cecil stood nearby by to act as a buffer between her and the dark side of magic because the temptation grew stronger every time Kit walked along the narrow line separating the light and dark sides of magical power. She'd finally come to realize their concern wasn't because they questioned her integrity—it was because they knew how easy it would be to simply become too exhausted to fight it and be caught in the vortex and sucked away from everything she loved and believed in.

When she'd questioned why the temptation didn't appear to challenge Braden, Cecil had laughed quietly and assured her that his test would come. Cecil had calmly explained, "We are all tested, Kit. Each of us has our mettle tested at least once—most of us several times during our lives. How we meet those challenges—the choices we make determine when and if we are tested again. Each test strengthens or weakens something within us. It is not ours to question the process, we need only meet the tests head-on, choose wisely and then use the newfound power we've earned in a way that makes the world a better place."

Later, as she'd mulled over Cecil's words, Kit realized they were reflected in the basic tenants of almost every one of the world's religions. It made perfect sense since the magical world drew its power from the Universe, but having it spelled out so clearly had been a defining moment for her as a witch. And now, letting the energy of the earth flow through her, Kit watched as the scene seemed to build itself piece by piece in her mind, but this time she didn't feel like she was standing alone in that cavern. As they'd promised, Cecil and her grandmother were by her side. She glanced to each side and was startled to see they were solid forms, unlike Braden who was only present in spirit—just as she was. Her grandmother's voice moved though her mind like a soft summer breeze, *"Remember your part. Don't deviate from the plan, no matter what you see or hear. Everything comes down to this moment—do exactly as you've been asked to do and always remember…I love you."*

Before Kit could respond, the grandmother she adored turned away from her. The sound of Sanskrit chants filled the space and Kit watched in horror as the wizard and Granny Good Witched stepped into the dimly lit open space. The rock surrounding the seal looked as if someone had been jack hammering it—even though there hadn't been a lot of progress made, Kit could see the granite was being pulverized and falling to the floor as she watched. It didn't take her long to notice the amount of dust falling softly to the floor was proportional to the intensity of the chants, and that explained why her granny and Cecil were so intent on interrupting the group gathered there.

Braden's strength infused her and she could feel her

mates pulling power from the earth as they let it course freely through their bodies to infuse in hers. Pushing her hands further in front of her, Kit began repeating the spell she'd been practicing for the past few days without any measurable success. But this time, she immediately felt the difference as the ground around her seemed to shift. Fighting to stay focused rather than worry about the confrontation she could see taking place in front of her, Kit closed her eyes and continued casting the spell.

When she finally opened her eyes, she was horrified by what she saw. As her concentration lagged, Kit felt the shaking ground begin to settle before Braden's harsh demands to focus filled her mind. *'No, we have to stay focused, Kit.'* Even though she didn't close her eyes, Kit used every bit of her concentration to push the power they were giving her into the spell. As the enormous boulders fell between the shadows where she and Braden were hidden and where the others stood, the dust and debris soon blocked her view. She hadn't seen Devin, but she could feel his presence as he added his power when hers started to lag.

Kit felt the energy draining from her and fought to hold on as long as possible. When she finally collapsed she felt strong arms lifting her just as the edges of her vision began to dim. The blackness raced to a center point and the din of crashing rocks began to fade, and then there was nothing but blissful silence.

🐾 🐾 🐾

TREV FELT AS if his whole body was numb. Watching as Cecil and Ruby were consumed by the avalanche of boulders, he felt the moment Kit's focus had faltered. And he'd also felt her renewed commitment to the task even as her heart had been torn to bits by what she'd seen. Jameson had caught their mate as she'd collapsed from sheer exhaustion and all three Michaels were tending to Braden, and he was shocked to see Marcus, his arm around Devin's shoulders, as he spoke to his brother quietly. He felt them all moving back to the estate's main house and almost immediately Trev was surrounded in nothing but the soft sounds of nature and his own harsh breaths.

Trev was still on his hands and knees gasping for breath, his head pounding as if it would explode when he felt soft, cool fingers smooth over his forehead. He hadn't even realized he'd closed his eyes until he turned into the touch looking to see whose touch was soothing his pain, but there wasn't anyone there. Blinking, he looked again and that was when he saw a faint mist outline and knew immediately who had touched him.

"Mom?" He watched in wonder as she reached for him and once again he felt her distinct touch and the unmistakable leaching of the pain pounding through his head. Closing his eyes at the relief, he felt more than saw her smile. When he reopened his eyes, Trev could feel his fathers' presence even though there wasn't anything to indicate they were also actually nearby.

'She's perfect for you, just as we knew she'd be. We are so proud of the men you have become—the leadership you exhibit, the compassionate way you care for those around you. But most of all we are proud of you as husbands and fathers. There is no greater joy for a parent than knowing their children have learned how to love.'

When he felt her presence start to fade, his strangled "Don't go, please, just a bit longer" sounded desperate, but he didn't care.

'I'm never far away, your fathers and I are always nearby. Playing with our grandchildren is far too tempting.' Her soft laughter filled his heart with joy and for the first time since he'd lost them, his heart didn't ache when he thought about all he'd lost. *'Go to her and let her know we are so proud of her, too. And assure her that things are not always as they appear.'*

Before he could ask her what she'd meant, Trev felt a cool breeze move over him and knew without even looking around that she was gone. Staggering to his feet, Trev only managed to take a few steps before pack members surrounded him.

Chapter Eighteen

Jameson was certain he'd never felt as helpless as he had while holding Kit after what had happened in front of the lab. She had awoken before they'd reached the house and her shattered cries had broken his heart. The grief pouring from her was almost tangible and he'd felt her overwhelming sorrow even before Trev had made his way to the house and explained what had happened. Jameson had known his brother was holding something back, but he'd been so focused on calming Kit down that he hadn't had time to ask any questions. They'd finally asked Angie to sedate their mate and that decision still tore him apart. What sort of mate was he—hell, what sort of Alpha was he that he couldn't comfort his own wife? The woman held his heart in the palm of her hand and he hadn't been able to reach her, hadn't been able to soothe her broken heart and it was killing him.

"It's not your fault, Jameson. She'd put everything she had into it and there just wasn't anything left in her to cope with what she'd seen. Kit is stronger than any of us can begin to imagine, she'll be okay—maybe not today, or even tomorrow, but she *will* bounce back." Angie stood beside him and Jameson could feel her studying him with an intensity that he might have found unnerving any other time.

"I hope to hell you are right, because I'm not sure I'll

survive feeling her break apart in my arms again." It had nearly destroyed him feeling her pain and not being able to bring her even the smallest measure of peace. After hearing Trev and Braden recount what had taken place, Jameson knew guilt and grief combined were going to take a long time to heal. "Is Trev still sleeping?" His brother had barely been conscious when he'd been carried into their suite. Jameson had put the two of them side by side in their bed knowing they'd seek the warmth and comfort of one another in their sleep.

"Yes. I've checked him over, physically he is fine—just completely drained. I'm not sure why he suffered from the energy drain more than you did, but he is almost as exhausted as she is."

Jameson turned to his cousin and saw the questions in her eyes, even though she hadn't asked them directly he owed her an explanation. "The gift our mother promised him is the ability to feel what Kit feels and see through her eyes when the situation warrants it." He saw Angie's eyes widen in surprise and he nodded. "He isn't sure it's much of a gift, but I'm in hopes he'll find a way to use it that honors our mother's memory. Hell, I can't even imagine how painful it had to have been to feel Kit's heart breaking—and I don't want to know." Breathing out a sigh, Jameson could only hope that Kit's parents would be able to help. He'd put out an emergency call to them, but wasn't sure how long it would take them to respond.

🐾 🐾 🐾

TREV STRETCHED AS he began to surface from the respite of sleep and felt Kit snuggled close at his side. As his mind came more fully awake his heart was once again weighed down when the memories of what he'd seen replayed in his mind. Before he could fall into a pit of worry he felt the same cool breeze brush over his cheek that he'd felt when his parents had moved around him outside the lab and he smiled at the familiarity of it. Opening his eyes, he looked around, and even though he didn't see anything, he was still filled with an unexplained peace as he remembered his mother's message for Kit. He'd thought his sweet mate was still sleeping until he heard her sniff.

Turning to his side, he pulled her against his chest and kissed the top of her head. He didn't speak for several minutes, there really wasn't much to say as she purged some of her grief with silent sobs. His heart was breaking for her, but until she'd had a chance to wash away some of the heartache with tears, Trev knew she wasn't going to be ready to hear his mother's message—ambiguous as it was.

Trev looked up to see Jameson standing in the doorway, his arms crossed over his bare chest and his face creased with worry. *'Is she alright? Do I need to get Angie?'*

'No, she is settling now. Please stay, I want you to hear what I have to say.' Trev saw the worry flash in his brother's expression, so he continued. *'I saw Mom, she was there after you left.'* Jameson's eyes widened and Trev could see his surprise.

'Fuck, did you get hit on the head? Hell, maybe I should call Angie for you.' Trev grinned because he knew his twin was trying to cover his shock with sarcasm, and if their positions were reversed he might well do the same. *'I'll order something for us to eat, our mate has to be running on empty. I'm anxious talk to Braden again and she also needs to hear his version of what happened, so I doubt she'll eat much but we need to try.'* Trev watched him move from the room and heard him speaking on the phone.

"Come on, baby. We need to get you cleaned up and dressed so we can talk before chaos erupts again." God what he'd give for a few weeks kicking back on some secluded beach watching his family play in the warm sunshine—letting it recharge all of their souls. Sighing to himself, Trev let the fantasy slide away. He hated moving her, but letting her sink into despair wasn't an option either. By the time they'd both cleaned up and dressed, their food had arrived. He and Jameson watched as she nibbled absently at the sandwich and shoved her favorite salad around on her plate. Her eyes were bleak and her face so pale that her skin appeared almost translucent.

Jameson leaned forward and covered her trembling hand with his, compassion filling his gaze, "Kitten, I've talked to Braden, but I'd also like to hear from you what happened." She nodded slowly. "I know you are completely spent, but I'd like to do this before any of the details slip from your memory. One of the first things I'd like to know is where exactly this cavern is. Since you were projecting yourself, I'm certain it could be anywhere in the world, but there was some unexplained seismic activity in our area today so I'm curious."

Trev was pleased that Jameson had chosen to begin their discussion with a question that didn't have any emotional components for Kit. It was moments like this that Trev could clearly see his twin's gift for leadership. The fact he'd instinctively known what direction to take was impressive.

"It is close...amazingly so, actually. But it's also very, very deep beneath the surface. The good thing is there won't be any way anyone will be able to make their way to the seal. The chanting was eroding the rock surrounding it, I watched it being slowly eaten away—falling to the stone floor as a fine dust. They hadn't made much progress, but they would have been able to loosen then remove the seal given enough time." Kit straightened in her chair and Trev watched in awe as she seemed to pull strength from the air surrounding her. Her posture straightened and her eyes cleared as she continued, "I didn't fully realize it at the time, but Damian was screaming at me from the other side to stop. He was crazed—calling out to Braden as well, but Braden never faltered. That young wizard never lost a moment's concentration, despite the fact he was losing a man he loved with everything he had. I could feel his determination to protect all of us, but his love for Angie, Trent, and Nick was his driving force." A single tear breached the bottom lid of her eyes and raced one another to her trembling chin.

Trev and Jameson each reached forward to swipe away the tear on their side before placing a soft kiss over the damp track. The tension that had made its way back into her body slowly ebbed away. Taking a deep breath, she continued, "Never doubt his loyalty to our pack. He's lost so many people he has loved, but he didn't hesitate to let the rocks fall around a man he loved so he could protect us all. I can't even imagine having to make such a decision at his age." *'She doesn't see that she possesses that same strength—that her loss was even greater than Braden's.'* Jameson's thoughts filled Trev's mind, echoing his own.

"What can you tell me about the people who were chanting?" Jameson looked between them both and Trev wondered how much Kit was going to be willing to reveal. He hadn't recognized any of them, but he was certain their mate had.

"There were several there that I have seen, but didn't know personally. They weren't particularly power—either in the political arena of the magic world or in their magical abilities, but they were adding power to those who were actually able to chisel away at the stone holding the seal in place." Trev watched as her eyes darkened with fury, "The ones I recognized are—well, *were* very powerful witches and wizards. Two of them were on the Supreme Council." She took a steadying breath and looked between them before whispering, "I thought Granny Good Witch and Cecil were along to make sure I wasn't tempted by the darkness—but that wasn't it at all. They were there to catch the traitors or at least to make sure they died for their actions, even though it cost them their own lives."

When the tears started again, Trev pulled her onto his lap and rocked her as she cried. This time he didn't curse the gift his mother had given him—this time he simply tried to absorb as much of her sadness as he could. The more of it he was slowly able to shift to himself, the less burden he felt weighing her down, and for the first time the *gift* actually seemed to more than a curse. As an earthbound creature, he would easily be able to disperse the grief simply by taking a punishing run through the woods. His wolf would simply pull positive energy from beneath his feet to erase the negative.

Making their way downstairs, Jameson was pleased to see the meeting room filled with the members of their pack. Kit was quickly swept away from his side by friends wanting to express their sympathy and those simply wanting to share their favorite stories about Ruby. By the time they'd finished briefing everyone, Kit's eyes were drifting closed as exhaustion once again claimed her.

🐾 🐾 🐾

THE FIRST THING Jameson did after everyone adjourned was clear his schedule for the next few weeks. His mate was quickly approaching her mating season and there wouldn't be much accomplished during that time except fucking her, and he didn't intend to miss a moment's time with her. She would also need their undivided attention while she tried to process the loss she'd suffered, hell, everyone at the estate was mourning Ruby's loss. Trev had relayed their mother's message, but it was so vague it really hadn't been any comfort to anyone. Jameson had sat back watching as Kit smiled and nodded, but she hadn't seemed moved by the words and he couldn't say that he blamed her.

The only loose end he planned to follow up on was bringing Libby Wells on board. Her scare at the university had probably worked in their favor and even though he was convinced the danger was likely over for now, her friendship with Kit would probably put her in harm's way again. He'd suggested that Charlie and Dirk make some much-needed improvements to their house, and both men had immediately begun making plans. He didn't doubt the pint-sized whirlwind would keep them all on their toes, but he was determined to make sure she was safe while she and Angie worked. The two of them were going to make history—he could feel it as if he'd almost been able to see the future. And who knew—perhaps his parents were speaking to him from the other side as well.

Leaning back in his chair, he smiled when Tristan Michaels stepped into the room. "Where is your mate?" Jameson almost smiled at the pained look on Tristan's face. Angie had always been an early riser, before Jameson had moved her back to the safety of the estate, she'd have already been on her way to the hospital by this time and the sun was just now sending golden orange rays shooting above the horizon.

"Sleeping peacefully—and she needs her rest." Tristan's sly smile confirmed what Jameson had already suspected.

"I walked past her in the hallway yesterday. Congratulations." Jameson didn't have to explain how he'd known Angie was pregnant—Tristan would already know her scent alone would have given away their news. This time Tristan's smile lit up his entire face, he and Nick had been trying to get their mate to "settle down" and start a family for several years. Jameson congratulated him and they both laughed about how round the petite pediatrician was going to be by the time summer rolled around. Angie was a shameless water baby and always had been—the only time she seemed to enjoy her down time was when she could lay in the warm sunshine beside the pool laughing and joking with her friends.

"She thought about the pool last night and it set her off on a tirade. She swears Nick and I 'knocked her up' deliberately so she'd be round as a beach ball. Of course Braden's offer to paint her belly with bright stripes didn't do much to calm her down. I finally had to threaten to paddle her ass at the next pack meeting to get her settled down. Hell, every time she gets upset she throws up—you'd think she'd learn." Jameson wanted to laugh out loud—hell, Dr. Angie Wolf-Michaels might be a lot of things, but calm wasn't likely to ever be one of them.

"Angie did ask if she could help plan a memorial service for Ruby. We know you'll be *busy* for a week or so, but we'd like to erect a small stone marker out back. We could dedicate it in a small ceremony whenever Kit is ready."

Jameson felt his heart constrict with emotion and he had to clear his throat in order to speak around the lump that was now lodged there. "Thank you—I don't know what else to say, except I'm grateful for all you've done for Kit and I know Trevlon is as well. And knowing the three of you will be taking care of the memorial takes the burden from Trev's and my shoulders. We'd mentioned it to Kit, but hadn't made any real plans." Just as he opened his mouth to say more, Kit's scent hit him full force and he was on his feet, moving before his mind even registered that he'd stood.

Tristan was already laughing as Jameson hit the door at a dead run. He hurdled the banister of the large stairway and was bounding up the stairs three at a time when he heard the distinctive sounds of his mate's pleasure. He left a trail of clothes through their suite, his cock was rock hard by the time he launched himself onto the bed. The scent of his mate in heat was quickly pushing rational thought out of his head. They'd enjoy a run under the full moon later tonight—probably a lot later. If they had enough energy, but for right now, their bed was the perfect place to begin working on a cousin and playmate for Angie's baby.

Epilogue

Kit stood outside in the cool misty morning looking down at the engraved marble marker in front of the lab where she and her granny had shared so many laughs. She could hardly believe it had been a month since she'd lost her colorful grandmother. She missed the high top wearing witch with the lightening quick wit more and more each day. She'd wanted to come out early and share a few quiet moments alone before everyone else joined her. Kit was still fuming that her parents had yet to show up—how her mom could be so callous, she simply couldn't imagine.

There had been nights when the scene in the cavern played over in Kit's mind until she was convinced she would go mad. The weeks she'd been in heat had been a blessed distraction, even if it had left her completely exhausted. Running under the full moon and fucking in the meadow until she hadn't had the strength to run home had helped too. Smiling to herself, she thought back on how her mates had been forced to shift back into their human form so they could carry her home. They'd taken her so many times her limbs had been as useless as overcooked noodles—there hadn't been a chance in hell she could make it home under her own steam. Well, may "been forced to" might be a bit harsh considering the fact they were still bragging about it to anyone who would listen.

Staring down at the small monument, she laughed at the multi-colored stones embedded in the rock of the high tops. The multi-faceted stones would glisten in the sun making them appear to shimmer and sparkle just like her granny's always had. Squatting down in front of the marker, Kit ran her fingers over the engraving, "Those who give selflessly sparkle in our memories forever."

Kit stood back up and fought back the tears that threatened to fall. Damn, she was just sure she was pregnant again and that meant she was going to be weepy for months. "And just when I was thought I'd cried all the tears I could. But it really is so perfect."

"I agree. It's cute as a button. Who's it for?" Kit froze. She was completely stunned for several long seconds, and then she was too afraid to turn her head and look. Too terrified that her mind was playing a cruel trick on her, that her soul deep desire to keep her grandmother close was making her hallucinate. "Kit? What's this about?"

When Kit turned to see Granny Good Witch standing at her side looking completely perplexed, Kit couldn't hold back the hysterical laughter that bubbled up from deep in her chest. All the stress of the past few weeks melted away and she felt her knees shaking. "Oh my Goddess—" was all she managed to get out before she wrapped her arms around her granny, hugging her tight. "How? I saw all the rocks falling. How? You and Cecil were with the people chanting and then you disappeared in the dust beneath the avalanche of boulders."

"Oh, that. No, we took them into custody and transported them back to the council chambers—which was kind of ironic since two of them were Supreme Council members. We might not have managed to get them out if your mother hadn't shown up just in time to help. You know how she likes to make an entrance." Her granny rolled her eyes like an errant teenager and Kit giggled.

"My mom was there?" Kit couldn't believe she'd seen so much, but missed just as much.

"Yeah, but damn she sure did cut it close. She'll be late for her own funeral, just you wait and see." For the first time, her granny looked up at her, shock etching her features. "Hey, why the tears? And you look like hell, sweetheart. Why so sad?"

Kit felt the hysteria building again as her entire body began to tremble. A warm muscular arm wrapped around her from behind anchoring her to an equally warm chest. *Trev.* "Nice to see you, Ruby, I have to say, you gave us all a hell of a scare. Where have you been?"

"Hi, Trev, what do you mean? I've been helping get those traitors settled in prison. Damn they have compromised a lot of projects the Supreme Council had been working on, but we'll get it all sorted out."

"We?" Kit was finally recovering enough that she was starting to feel the beginnings of a real good tantrum building.

"Well, there were two openings on the Council, and your mom and I have both been asked to fill those seats." With a quick wave of her hand, Ruby was wearing deep purple robes and her high tops were covered in glittering amethysts and alexandrite stones. "I wanted something a little flashier, but your mother has become a regular stick in the mud. I don't know who appointed her the fashion police of the Council, but I'm stuck with one color—for now." Her wink let Kit know the Supreme Council was probably never going to know a dull moment while Granny Good Witch was a member.

Before Kit could ask any more questions, they were

surrounded by family and friends who were thrilled to see Ruby standing in the midst of what was supposed to have been a memorial service in her honor. When Cecil showed up a few minutes later, Braden let out a whoop and threw himself in the elderly wizard's arms. Kit wasn't sure which of them shed more tears or which one tried to hide them more.

It was Braden who finally broke the tension, "Wow, how cool is it that you get to attend your own funeral—well sort of at least." Cecil and Granny Good Witch high-fived each other as everyone adjourned to the mansion for breakfast.

Kit had hung back with Jameson and Trev, she just couldn't seem to stop staring at the memorial. "Even though she is still with us, I feel like I've been changed forever by this experience. And I keep remembering your mother's message and how right she was—that things certainly weren't as they seemed."

Turning to face them, Kit was overwhelmed for a moment at the enormity of the blessing she'd received when Fate led her into their downtown club. She felt the first tear trail down her cheek and their knowing smiles almost made her groan. "You are so beautiful, kitten. You take my breath away."

"And knowing that you are carrying our child—well, that makes everything even more perfect." Trev trailed his fingers up and down the inside of her arm causing her to tremble. "Everyone will be busy celebrating for a while—I don't think we'd be missed for an hour—or two." Kit felt moisture rush to her sex and hoped they managed to find a private place to play—quickly.

As they moved her quickly into the small bedroom at the back of the lab, Kit didn't even try to hold back her joyous giggle because this would probably be one of the most successful experiences she'd ever had in the small building she'd blown up more than once and almost burned down more times than she wanted to remember. *Oh yeah, I'm going to watch something blow up and I fully intend to set a couple of hot shifters on fire—yes, indeed—this lab is about to finally fulfill its destiny.*

The End

Books by Avery Gale

The Wolf Pack Series
Mated – Book One
Fated Magic – Book Two
Tempted by Darkness – Book Three

Masters of the Prairie Winds Club
Out of the Storm
Saving Grace
Jen's Journey
Bound Treasure
Punishing for Pleasure
Accidental Trifecta
Missionary Position

The ShadowDance Club
Katarina's Return – Book One
Jenna's Submission – Book Two
Rissa's Recovery – Book Three
Trace & Tori – Book Four
Reborn as Bree – Book Five
Red Clouds Dancing – Book Six
Perfect Picture – Book Seven

Club Isola
Capturing Callie – Book One
Healing Holly – Book Two
Claiming Abby – Book Three

I would love to hear from you!

Email:
avery.gale@ymail.com

Website:
www.averygalebooks.com/index.html

Facebook:
facebook.com/avery.gale.3

Instagram:
avery.gale

Twitter:
@avery_gale

Excerpt from Out of the Storm

Masters of the Prairie Winds Club
Book One
by Avery Gale

TOBI STROBEL WAS livid...completely over the top pissed. From the moment she'd burst into her boss's office at Austin Gardens and Homes and met Lilly West, her entire world had seemed to tip on its axis. Tobi had been on a tear about the interview she'd been trying to schedule with Prairie Winds "cad" owners, Kyle and Kent West. And she hadn't even bothered to knock before she'd blown into the small room like a Cat 5 hurricane. When the beautiful dark haired beauty had introduced herself as the "cads" mother, Tobi had wanted to melt into the floor. But Lilly West had been the epitome of grace and only laughed as she'd agreed that her sons were a handful for sure, even though she claimed to be withholding judgment on the "cad" determination. Tobi had felt drawn to Lilly in a way she hadn't really been able to explain, and the only reason she could come up with was because she'd lost her own mother when she'd been so young. The excuse sounded weak even in her own mind, but it was the only reason she could come up with...at least it was the only one she was willing to accept. Lilly had assured Tobi that her assessment of Kyle and Kent avoiding interviews was dead on and had promised to help her secure an appointment the following day. Before Lilly had left the small magazine's office, she'd given Tobi a long hug and then kissed her on the forehead saying, "They are going to be thrilled to finally find you."

Later that night Tobi had laid awake wondering at the woman's strange words, but her musings had been cut short by a text message from Kent West giving her directions to Prairie Winds and asking her to arrive at precisely seven the next evening. Tobi hadn't minded the fact she'd be giving up her Friday evening because she never really went out anyway. It wasn't like she had any disposable funds for entertainment, and quite frankly, her small apartment wasn't in a neighborhood that was safe to be out and about in after dark. What she hadn't planned on was the fact she'd be facing a storm so fierce she'd been forced to pull over to the edge of the road because she hadn't been able to see where she was going.

Thank God she'd left her seat belt fastened because she had no sooner put her small car in park than a large truck had barreled past and barely clipped her back bumper, sending her ancient Toyota nose down into a deep ditch. The ditch was rapidly filling with water, so Tobi grabbed her things, wrapped them in a couple of plastic bags she found under her seat and climbed back up to the roadside. Amazingly, not one single person had stopped despite the fact she'd been standing right at the road's edge.

The next time she'd seen lights headed her way, she'd moved to the center of the road and had begun waving her arms wildly over her head. Just as the enormous black pickup had gotten close, a bolt of lightning hit in the field to her right and the flash had illuminated the startled expression of a man Tobi could only describe as movie star handsome. She'd only gotten a glimpse of his dark intensity before she'd found herself jumping to the side to keep from becoming his newly mounted hood ornament. By the time he'd managed to screech to a stop, she was hopping mad and stalking toward the large black pickup as fast as her short legs would carry her. She was only five foot two, but as she liked to remind those around her, what she lacked in size, she made up for in attitude.

Tobi had almost reached his truck by the time he finally stepped out, "You almost ran over me. Holy smokes Batman you could have killed me with that monstermobile of yours. Damn, a drowned rat. My whole life is spiraling out of control faster than a Kardashian marriage I tell ya. Shit, shit, double shit. My car is probably floating toward the lake and my stuff is in trash bags. *Trash bags!* That's a whole new level of the wrong side of the tracks, even for me. I'm so wet I'm pretty sure I won't be dry for a month of Sundays, hell's fire I'll probably mold. And you are freaking huge and probably some serial killer on the top of some most wanted list. I'll end up on the evening news and my brother will never even know what happened to me because he refuses watch the damned news. My crazy ass neighbors will pick apart my apartment before the broadcast is even over and I'll be a footnote on some unsolved mysteries show a few years from now. And I still don't know what Lilly West meant by finding me. Damnation this sucks big green donkey dicks I'm telling ya for sure." When she finally came up for air and realized the tall hunk in front of her was simply staring at her with his mouth in a grim line, all she could manage to do was blush. He had to be at least a foot taller than she was and his dark hair was barely visible under the Stetson he was wearing. His eyes were a deep chocolate brown that was quickly turning even darker. She realized she was staring at him just as he spoke.

"How do you know my mother?" Mr. Tall, Dark and Intimidating demanded.

Did he just say mother? That's it...that is the final straw. I'm officially certifiable and straitjacket ready. "Mother? Lilly West is your mother?" Looking up at the sky, she asked, "You're kidding me, right, God? First, you put their mom in my boss's office just as I have a meltdown about the infamous kink masters not returning my calls. And then of all the people on this planet, you let me almost get run over by one of the men I've been trying to schedule a meeting with for weeks? Is this some kind of a joke?" Just as the words left her mouth the world around them exploded in light and a crash of thunder that was so immediate she was sure the bolt must have hit right beside them. *Holy shit! Reminder to self...do not challenge the Big Guy.*

"Get in the truck, *now.*" His words had been more growled than spoken and ordinarily she'd be giving him a piece of her mind for thinking he could give her orders, but right now she was more afraid of becoming a crispy critter in the middle of the highway than she was of Lilly West's son. Tobi briefly wondered whether he was Kyle or Kent as she scrambled into the big black beast when he opened the door and motioned her inside, but judging by his clipped tone she was guessing Kyle.

She'd done her homework on the owners of Prairie Winds because she'd been hoping to interview them since she first heard about the BDSM club they were building just a few minutes from her home. Sure, she worked for a magazine that spotlighted all things bright and beautiful in the Austin area, but in truth, her interest in the club was much more personal. Banishing those thoughts for the moment, she turned and plopped her soggy ass in the passenger seat and turned to see him staring at her as if he'd never seen a woman before. *What the hell?*

Made in the USA
Coppell, TX
29 December 2021